Robin Llywelyn was born in 1958 and raised in Llanfrothen, Meirionnydd (now part of Gwynedd). He was educated at the University College of Wales, Aberystwyth. *White Star* is a translation of his first novel, *Seren Wen ar Gefndir Gwyn* (literally 'a white star against a white background') which won the National Eisteddfod Prose Medal at Aberystwyth in 1992. It also won the Arts Council of Wales Book of the Year Award and the Welsh Academy's John Griffith Williams Memorial Prize. It was published in French as *Étolie Blanche sur Fond Blanc* by Terre de Brume in 2003. His second novel, *O'r Harbwr Gwag i'r Cefnfor Gwyn* won the National Eisteddfod Prose Medal at Neath in 1994 and the BBC Writer of the Year Award the same year. It was published in English as *From Empty Harbour to White Ocean* by Parthian in 1996 and in Italian as *Da Porto Deserto a Bianco Oceano* by Piero Manni in 2000. A number of his short stories have been translated and published in Breton, English, French, German, Italian and Bulgarian.

Robin Llywelyn is a grandson of architect Clough Williams-Ellis. He has worked at Portmeirion since 1983 and is married with three children.

By the Same Author

Seren Wen ar Gefndir Gwyn
O'r Harbwr Gwag i'r Cefnfor Gwyn
Y Dŵr Mawr Llwyd
Published by Gwasg Gomer

Places. Y Man a'r Lle 1: Llanfrothen
Published by Gwasg Gregynog

Portmeirion published by Portmeirion Ltd.

White Star

Robin Llywelyn

Translation in collaboration with Gwen Davies

Originally published in Welsh as *Seren Wen ar Gefndir Gwyn* by Gwasg Gomer
on behalf of the National Eisteddfod of Wales, 1992

This translation first published in 2004 by
Parthian
The Old Surgery
Napier Street
Cardigan
SA43 1ED
www.parthianbooks.co.uk

ISBN 1-902638-31-X

Typeset in Sabon

Printed and bound by Dinefwr Press, Llandybïe

With Support from the Parthian Collective

Edited by Gwen Davies

Parthian is an independent publisher that works with the support of the
Arts Council of Wales and the Welsh Books Council

A cataloguing record for this book is available from the British Library

Cover Art: Cwm Bleiddiaid by Elfyn Lewis
Cover Design: Marc Jennings

I Sian

Special thanks to Gwen Davies for her work in editing and collaborating on the translation.

The Clerk Zählappell had hardly slept a wink so it was little wonder he was groggy going about his work in Entwürdigung Castle's Screen Archives that morning. Probably this was why he entered the wrong code into the word box and got three cards in his inbox instead of the one he'd been expecting.

"How can I get rid of these now?" he asked himself. He knew there was no chance of getting back into the source file without leaving a trace. He took them home in his little black briefcase. Back to his garret at the top of the tall terrace that faces the River Häfling in the shadow of the castle. He picked at a cold supper. On automatic pilot he loaded the cards into his screen player and blindly watched the green light as it splintered into a red flashing copyright warning: "RESTRICTED ACCESS. EMPIRE WAR ARCHIVE." But Zählappell was already dozing peacefully in his armchair as the words rolled slowly up the screen:

Testimony One

It was after the paper revolution, on the night we gained our freedom, that my troubles started. Town Square had been chock-a-block all afternoon and by evening the pubs were overflowing into the streets. I was too busy watching out for you crossing the street somewhere to take much notice of so-and-so's understated smile or whatisname's finger pointing my way. None of it really registered until Dave Egg Stealer planted his elbow in my ribs and winked his wink at me. It wasn't just the high spirits of the evening shining in his eyes.

"Still free as a bird then," was all he said.

"What are you blabbering on about?" But he was gone, sunk back into the crowd. Having dossed around a bit longer listening to the speeches blaring out of the megaphones strung along the towers around the square, and no whisky left to keep me warm, I pulled up my collar around my ears and set off somewhere. I did mean to call on you at Helen's Stone, Caress, but how could I even start to explain now that our words have turned to weapons? I was down in the underpass when I saw Scarlet Nightshade; there she was crouched down, crying her heart out, hair across her teeth and a bruise spreading on her cheek. She was picking up some small beads that were strewn about the concrete.

"What happened, Scarlet?" I said lightly. I had struck up a chat with her earlier over on Town Square, but I'm not keen on her; she's always on the verge of some crisis.

"Just leave me alone," she said fixing me with tiger's eyes. Her mascara was in dark streams down her cheeks. Scarlet Nightshade can be a wild one; you wouldn't want to get on the wrong side of her.

"But, Scarlet... it was only..."

"Just go," she spat. "Go back to your Little Caress Heart, and see if she'll take you in."

I turned for home. There's no point tangling with such a spiteful girl.

Outside All Night Café Wil Pickled Herring was sitting on the pavement with his head in his hands. I couldn't make out a word he said to me, not even when he showed his ugly black-pegged smile and slowly drew his forefinger across his throat. All I did was step in past him to get something to eat.

"Let's have something to warm me up, Betsan," I said to Betsan Ten Minutes behind the counter. "How's the new job going?"

"You can have hot stew and mind your own business."

The word on the street is that Betsan Ten Minutes is getting it regular off Wynne Screen Viper nowadays so that's why she's working nights behind the counter at All Night Café and not upstairs on her back anymore. Then the door opens and back comes Wil Pickled Herring hanging on it like a rock-climber. He lost his grip and fell all over the tables.

"Out!" shouted Betsan Ten Minutes grabbing a mop handle and whacking him on his back and shoulders. Wil Pickled Herring didn't move a muscle. She flung the mop at him and left him in a heap. She came back behind the counter and looked me up and down. "Surprised to see you're still around," she said.

"I've had it up to here," I protested. "Could you just tell me why everyone is suddenly so interested in my whereabouts; what's going on?"

"They were here just now looking for you."

"Who were?"

"They're after you, Gwern, didn't you know? I didn't tell them anything, mind."

"What the hell could you tell them? Why would they be looking for me?" Betsan Ten Minutes is known for winding people up and digging the dirt on them, so she didn't take me in. Just then Wil

4

Pickled Herring pulled himself up at my table and began to dribble and ramble and pull faces so I gave Betsan two units for the food and split. Who knows, maybe I was expecting something, but I went straight home anyway. My stomach turned as soon as I saw the answer machine with its red eye flashing. First I'd opened the note I'd found on the mat. I suppose I hadn't taken much notice of the news lately or the new world order we were living in. Nothing much had changed in town and anyway I'd been working away a lot so I suppose I wasn't quite up to speed at that stage.

"Jesus," I thought as I read the note. "It's true then; Fischermädchen does want to see me. Way things are going I'll be on a one-way ticket to Entwürdigung Castle and Rausman himself flaying the hide off my bones."

I clean forgot about the answer machine when I read that note; I just drummed out her number like a woodpecker on a tree-trunk.

Fischermädchen was not too happy to be woken in the middle of the night, but when she realised it was me she changed her tune.

"Gwern, at last! Where've you been?" she said, laying on the charm. "I've been waiting for your call."

"I know," I said. "I'll be round first thing in the morning, don't worry. Does this have anything to do with the network contract? Look, I did say beforehand that I wasn't too sure about that software.... Are they really angry?"

"Tomorrow morning, eight o'clock. Don't worry, Gwern. Come by eight, everything is fine."

I had heard Dave Egg Stealer talking about some Saffron Tinker or other, saying he was your man for crossing borders with asylum seekers fleeing from the Heartless Bodies. "He's the one I need," I told myself; he'll get me to Small Country. But then it struck my dumb skull, "No, no way will that work: he's just somebody from one of those new legends! He isn't even real so what's the bloody point?"

Even if I was thick enough to believe in this Saffron Tinker bloke, just like the children and the old people, I didn't have his access code and I couldn't have contacted him anyway without the Listeners getting straight onto my case. "If you can't be strong, be cunning," I told myself: what other options had I anyway?

I was well out of there; I just chucked whatever came to hand into a bag. Thought of phoning you; wised up fast. I flipped open the screen and deleted the log of restricted access files. Some files I tried to reopen just to check they were really gone. A quick message for Fischermädchen for forward delivery and I was tailing it hotfoot. Got a lift off Wil Califfornia to the station, didn't wait for change, jumped the fence and just about made it onto the night train.

"Ticket, son," says the guard.

"Haven't got one."

"Penalty charge then," he says.

"Swipe that, grandad," says I, thrusting my unit card at him. A little yellow paper ticket with the ink still wet squiggled out of a box on his belly.

I didn't get off where I was supposed to but carried on into the night, past places I'd never heard of. The night was like a long tunnel and the carriage lights lit up dozing passengers in their yellow glare. Some of the people were foreigners, some even from the Exile States. I held my face to the glass and watched raindrops running races down the pane outside. At Gwastadaros siding I slipped out into a blue dawn. It has a big name for a small place, the sign is huge but there are only a few unplastered concrete huts on the station. Even the searchlights keep going on and off just like ours. The people here are very much like we are back home: the first thing anyone said to me was "Where're you from? Going far?"

He was a taxi driver but he only took me a short distance.

"Small Country?" he said. "No chance, mate. I can't take you there. You'd better get out here, pronto."

"Bastard," I replied and gave him two fingers as he drove away. I started walking concrete roads but I couldn't figure out which way to go. It wasn't that cold but the sun was under cloud and there was drizzle in the breeze. I tried to make out where the sun would be if you could've seen it and walked in that direction. The main road rose from the station village up towards the hills, the east I hoped. Behind the hills a rampart of dark rock rose to meet the clouds. The concrete road got all pitted and crazed, every mile worse until the surface was like a net cast over a stony stream. An hour or so later, and hardly getting anywhere, I saw on the hill's edge above the road a little cottage like a holiday home but with a chimney smoking like a steamer. I went towards it, thinking to ask if I was lost. It was a fair distance away, but the longer I climbed the farther off the damn place went. I was sweating like a swine in a sauna when I finally made it to the farmyard, having wasted the best part of a day, and now night was falling on the second evening. Three ferocious dogs came at me, barking and baring their dripping fangs.

"Down, you brutes," I said, "or you'll get it."

They circled me snarling until a lanky youth with hollow cheeks came out of the cottage. He had a yellow cloak around him, a sack over his shoulder and thonged sandals on his feet. He started to pelt the dogs with stones from his sack while shouting in my direction, "Welcome to Sunless Summer!"

"Oh, that's a good one," I replied. "I've heard that story before; isn't the Saffron Tinker in that one?"

"You'd better come inside," said the sallow youth. "Bonebleach doesn't like to be kept waiting."

I followed him into the house, a dark smoke-filled place mouldy as moth-balls; the only modern stuff there was a green screen flickering in the corner. Bonebleach is a bloody big bloke, with a mop of curly red hair and a big red beard. I was given a steaming bowl of bread and milk and baked potatoes with butter. I wolfed it all down anyway.

"So what kept you?" he demanded when I'd finished. "You must've got the message?"

"Oh, yes, sure!" I blurted out. "Do you know the Saffron Tinker, sir?"

"What did you do, Gwern, to get the Heartless Bodies after you?"

"I did bugger all to them."

"Come on, sonny," said the big man. "Let's get real. Your case is hopping all over the network screen."

"Look," I said, afraid now, "it's Scarlet Nightshade who started this. She's turned Little Caress Heart against me and I wouldn't put it past her feeding poisonous titbits about me to Fischermädchen herself. Look, it was Wil Pickled Herring who broke her necklace and made her cry, not me!"

"And what's all this about you and the network crash in the Exile States? It's no wonder the Heartless Bodies are after you for wrecking the system! And by mistake as well, for God's sake; all down to incompetence, not patriotism at all! You'd deserve a bit more respect if you'd done it on purpose, you blundering idiot."

"It was on purpose, Mr Bonebleach, I swear! I wanted to spoil their plans, it wasn't an accident!"

"Bullshit! You're just a crap programmer."

"You can believe what you like," I sulked.

"That's better," he boomed. He's such a pompous man. "So you'd reckoned on escaping towards Small Country?"

"If you say so, Mr Bonebleach."

"I've seen plenty of the likes of you before."

"Is Small Country far?"

"Far from where, son? What a question!" Bonebleach beckoned to the lad. "Tell him how far it is to Small Country, Pilgrim."

"It's nearer than yesterday and further than tomorrow," said the sombre youth.

"Well you're all leaving tomorrow anyway," said Bonebleach.

"Is Saffron Tinker coming too, sir?" I inquired innocently.

"Know him, then, do you?"

"So he does exist? Everyone's heard the legends about him leading fugitives from the Heartless Bodies to Small Country!"

Bonebleach laughed at this and started to slap his knee with his palm. "Yes, very good," he said simmering with mirth. "Well, he is here, right enough, yes indeed. He's been waiting a long while for you, you three-legged snail."

"Sorry about that," I muttered.

"Tomorrow morning then; Saffron Tinker, Pilgrim World and you are to set off towards Small Country. Those are my orders from on high. Here's a mobile processor; keep it up to date, that's an order. Get some sleep, then be on your way: after that I couldn't give a monkey's."

"Thank you, sir," I said, taking the processor, not really knowing what he was on about or whether I'd any reason to thank him anyway.

Sunless Summer is a big country, vast I reckon. Some say it has no borders but I don't believe it. A country must stop somewhere or it can't be whole, surely? Well, anyway, I never saw such a wasteland as this place we were passing through. Rolling bare hills as far as the horizon and not so much as a furze bush growing. No walls. No paths. A country like the waves of the sea with no surf breaking. Had there been pasture it would have been a great place for sheep, but the few we saw were small and hungry, making a mean living off the odd grassy clump. But though there is no sun nor pasture, the people here greet you with a smile. I don't know where they live or what they do. We saw no houses. I doubt they get many visitors, or they wouldn't be half so hospitable. "Welcome to Sunless Summer!" they'd shout as hordes of ragged children came from nowhere, crowding around your legs and smiling into your face. Saffron Tinker just kept frowning like a scarecrow at everyone, his yellow eyes flashing disapproval in all directions. You'd have thought his wild appearance would be enough to frighten them, what with his stooped gait, long arms and spindly short legs leaping here and there. No question: he's a mean old git. Mind you, he was actually pretty decent to me during the journey. Now and then he'd let me get up behind him on his mule for a few miles. Pilgrim had to walk the whole way, poor sod.

"I prefer to walk" he'd say whenever I got a ride. "My destiny is to walk the rough paths forever; that is as it should be and ever shall be, and should there be no path left in this transient world I would still walk on in a circle like a mouse on a wheel."

I didn't know him well at that stage, tending to put his weirder statements down to wisdom. "But why d'you want to carry a sack full of stupid stones around with you?" I asked. "Aren't we surrounded by them here?"

"Listen, my lad," he said in a boastful voice, squaring his owl-like shoulders, "some people prefer to carry their weight on their backs rather than in their hearts. Anyway, these are special stones."

"When you two have finished quarrelling," said Saffron Tinker, "you can pitch camp on the ridge over there. It gets dark early on the borders of Wild Country."

So we were in Wild Country then. I'm not denying that it was cold, it was bloody cold; it hit you like a fist in the mornings and like a blade cutting through the mist at night. It would be no big deal for your eyelids to freeze shut, and I almost didn't recognize Dave Egg Stealer as he swaggered into camp towards me wrapped in his big coat.

"Hey, Gwern!" he shouted with a wink like the one he gave me on Town Square. "So you've arrived."

"Egg Stealer!" I cried. "What brought you here?"

"Keep your nose out," he said. "Sealed lips are sweet. I thought you'd had it back in town."

I told him about the hassle I'd had and all he did was laugh.

"Listen, Gwern," he said "both you know and I know that you weren't working with Small Country's Lower Level guys, so keep your fibs. It was an accident, end of story. You fouled up their systems good and proper, though, I'll give you that, you cack-handed bugger. I bet Fischermädchen's face was a picture when you wriggled out of her velvet mittens. You were always the lucky bastard!" He laughed heartily and slapped me on the back.

"Stuff your luck, Egg Stealer," I snapped. I couldn't see much to laugh about.

"Just you work on your story, my son."

"Why do they call it Wild Country, Egg Stealer?" I asked to change the subject.

"How the hell should I know?" he said. "Perhaps it's because the Wire Bandits rear all their Shining Beasts here."

"Are the Shining Beasts dangerous?"

"'Course not, they'd only tear you to shreds. They'd guzzle up six better men than you before breakfast. My advice: don't look them in the eye and they won't harm you. And don't even think about laying a finger on them or you'll have Rock Jaw, leader of the Wire Bandits to answer to."

Dave Egg Stealer went on his way. Going down to Sunless Summer, he said, with an important message for Bonebleach. That's what he said, anyway. But knowing Dave Egg Stealer he was probably just showing off. But fair play, he did lend me his restplate so I could carry on safely into the frozen wastes above. It was a good one too, a shiny transparent plate that fitted like a second skin. I gave him Saffron Tinker's mule in return because Dave Egg Stealer said that it would be no use to us in Wild Country; far too slippery on the rocks for a mule and so forth. Saffron Tinker was none too pleased when he found out what I'd done. Called me every name under the sun and threatened to throw me off the ledge and beat me with his stick but he was too frail so I broke it and offered to carry the tent and that sorted him out. But of course Saffron Tinker is a poor walker, his spindly legs have no strength, and we had to stay where we were for a while. I thought it was a good bargain because I would never have managed to sleep those nights in Wild Country without the restplate to protect me, what with the Shining Beasts howling and braying and stirring it up around the camp and eyeing our tent with their electric eyes as they churned up clumps of the mountain with their hooves until the night would turn into a wild storm of lightning all about us. Pilgrim had no restplate so he just lay there shivering in his cloak through the small hours without a wink of sleep, groaning and saying his prayers under his breath. Probably all part of his penance; being exposed to the elements meant he could suffer properly. Pilgrim is a strange fellow.

Of course Saffron Tinker would get into a blind fury with the Shining Beasts, the night shuddering with his screams and shouts. "Get out of here you blasted devils! There's nothing for you here! Clear off!" And he would reach for his combat claw and threaten them with it while shielding his eyes from their piercing gaze and they'd retreat behind the escarpment until Saffron Tinker had gone back to lie in the tent, and everything would be peaceful in the camp again. But little by little the Shining Beasts would creep back stealthily, stepping from shale to scrub and they'd strike up their unearthly crying and wailing while flashing their electric eyes and churning up the rocks with their hooves until the lightning storm filled the night and Saffron Tinker would erupt again, swearing and blinding like a devil and dancing and bounding like a man gone mad.

This is how it was for nights on end. Once in the belly of the night Saffron Tinker knotted a cord onto his combat claw and sped it towards the Shining Beasts until the claw caught in the flank of one of them. He pulled, the Shining Beast screamed, and the claw took the hide clean off the side of the moaning beast from its shoulder to its hind quarters. It was a terrible scene, with all the Shining Beasts crowding around the wounded one, howling and roaring and gnashing their teeth and flashing their eyes as the injured beast lay crying quietly on its side in a pool of blood on the rock. Eventually the herd turned tail and charged away beyond the escarpment and we weren't bothered by them again that night.

The next morning when I looked out from under the side of the tent, who did I see encircling the camp but the Wire Bandits mounted on Shining Beasts all around us, stony faced and with arms folded on their chests and their eyes staring mute at the wounded one lying in its own blood. All it could do was lick dew from the stones and roll its heavy eyes like marbles in its head. I shook Saffron Tinker to wake him, but that didn't work: I suppose he was too tired to wake after being kept up every night by the Shining Beasts.

"Saffron Tinker! Saffron Tinker! The Wire Bandits are here!" I cried giving him a tweak on his purple nose.

"Leave me alone you little weevil," he cried. The next minute he opened one big round yellow eye. "What did you say?"

"The Wire Bandits are here and they want to see you."

"Oh heavens, what will we do now?" said Pilgrim.

"Be quiet, you two," said Saffron Tinker. "I'll go out to them then, you useless cowards. Rock Jaw and I are thick as thieves. He eats out of my very hand, for God's sake. Really, he's not as unreasonable as some make out, no, not at all." He can be so brave, poor Saffron Tinker.

With that he wrapped his cloak about him and stepped out onto the camp ledge. I say camp but it was really hardly more than a tent and an open hearth on a level patch under the mountain's eaves.

I was watching from under the tent and Pilgrim World was watching with me and both of us quaking and the tent quivering as we saw old Saffron Tinker standing before the Wire Bandits and the bandits all closing in on him, with some even leaping from their Shining Beasts and pinioning him between them. Rock Jaw raised his hand.

"Saffron Tinker!" he said. "You have injured my Shining Beast through black treachery and his value I claim. Oh rude serf, you will pay the price of this insult!"

They bound old Saffron Tinker and flung him across the back of one of the Shining Beasts and then tied his wrists and ankles together to form a girth under the belly of the beast so that he couldn't even raise a hand to wave goodbye as they took him away.

As if in afterthought Rock Jaw stopped and turned his beast towards us in our hiding place. "And as for you two lurking in there, don't think this doesn't concern you too. You'd better make sure my beast gets well. Saffron Tinker can do its work in Switchback City until you bring this one back to me in full health and vigour. Do you understand!" And with that the warband galloped away from us, their streaming pennants glistening behind them and their wild long hair swimming in the wind and we weren't troubled by the Shining Beasts ever again.

"Bwwwww!" said the injured animal and we went to see what could be done to heal him. His flank was an open wound and despite the cold there were already maggots squirming in his flesh. We washed out the wound with melted snow. The beast snorted and dribbled but was too weak to struggle. Then Pilgrim World took from his sack some of his so-called special stones and carefully laid them on the beast's flank over the wound. We lit a fire to keep the creature warm and boiled water to make porridge to spoonfeed him. Our beast slept the whole night through without groaning or anything and the following morning he managed to raise his head from the moss we'd packed under his head as a pillow. His eyes had stopped rolling around like marbles in his head and he fixed us with a steady gaze.

"They should call you Gwern Medicine Man," said Pilgrim, "not Gwern Excuses." I told him I thought there might be something in his special stones after all.

We spent three weeks curing the beast and when he died we wanted to cry. We were gutted because we'd become best friends with the poor creature; he even used to lick our faces and blow warm air up our nostrils when we fed him.

"How shall we bury him? This ground is harder than Spanish iron!" Really, Pilgrim World is enough to drive anyone round the bend.

"Put the rest of your damned special stones over him for all

14

they're worth now," I said crossly, blaming him and his stupid stones for everything. But it was stones from the mountainside that we collected in the end because Pilgrim World refused to share any more of his own.

We left the tent where it was and struck out for the gap above where Saffron Tinker had shown the way to Small Country pass. We trudged on through clouds spiralling like cold smoke. At night Pilgrim had no choice but to share my restplate or he'd certainly have frozen solid. We'd no tent and his cloak was worn threadbare, we were on our last legs and our provisions were gone. The daytime kept shrinking smaller and smaller every day and the chill of the mountain kept closing around us tighter every night. We must have left Wild Country behind us by now and reached the middle of Bleak Winter because there was nothing but mist below us with outcrops of rock peeking through it like islands. The paths were all shale and ice and we'd lost our way completely. There is no colour in Bleak Winter, no trees, no birds. A stump of a day and then a cloak of night from mid-afternoon to mid-morning. On the last day Pilgrim World slumped down by the side of his sack like a wreath on a stone.

"My ears are bleeding and I've lost all feeling in my toes," he said. "I can't go on."

"Well, the pass won't come to us," I said accusingly.

"This is all my fault," said he.

"Yes," I said, "because you're the one who's supposed to know these bloody frozen rocks like a mountain goat, you spineless useless weakling."

A shower of hail was the next plague to strike us, rising like a swarm of angry bees over the clifftop below and pelting us until we cringed. We managed to crawl into a crack in the rock to shelter but the restplate was no use there. Pilgrim's stones didn't seem to be doing us much good either so I grabbed his sack and flung it over the edge of the precipice.

"You shouldn't have done that," said Pilgrim, his head hanging like a duck strung up outside the butcher's.

"Go to hell," I said as my eyes closed and my mind circled like a kestrel above a deep ravine.

It was a fine sunny ravine. I was falling and falling until my stomach was doing somersaults inside me and the earth was rising like a ball towards me and all the time I was trying to raise back my head to stop my fall before I hit the ground. But I landed like a feather after all, close to Helen's Stone. I was in the orchard, where the blossom boiled over in the apple trees and where the rolling green bracken was swept with warm insects in the sunlight and the cold smell of moss awoke in me a boy catching tiddlers in a jam jar from the stream. I went towards Helen's Stone and you opened the door and smiled and said nothing so I knew I was only dreaming. "It's cold in Bleak Winter, Caress," I said. "I know," you said, "I still love you and won't listen to Scarlet Nightshade's lies." I could smell flowers and sun as I watched your smile. "Why can't the dream last forever?" I said. "Nothing lasts forever, Gwern," you said, your voice so warm and gentle. "Will you be like this forever, Caress?" I said. "They're looking for you," you said and then you turned when the baby cried. The shadows were climbing like roses up the whitewashed wall, and the river was a murmur far away; the slate flags of the footpath were sinking beneath my feet as you smiled and raised your hand to wave goodbye but I couldn't move a muscle, not even to speak, as darkness surrounded me.

Testimony Two

They took us up to Small Country on the backs of mules, once they'd got us going again by rubbing us with some leaves very like dock leaves, except that they stung like nettles.

"We are the masters of Bleak Winter," the Swarthy Cavedwarves told us. "We'll get a good price for a couple of ruffians like you from Grind Underfoot."

They tied our feet under the bellies of the mules and our arms about their necks, to stop us falling into the void below, they said. Dave Egg Stealer's story about the path being unsuitable for mules was a pack of lies. They took us away through the day and through the night with flaming torches lighting up our way.

At daybreak one morning I knew we were close. We hadn't seen birds of any kind since leaving Sunless Summer but now I could see some black birds like ravens circling above and cawing. It made me think we must be getting nearer. For once I was right. The mules struggled over boulders, my face was tight against the rough mane, but still I glimpsed a gap in the mountain wall before us and caught the smell of burning bracken through the thin air. We entered the valley from above and zig-zagged down to the flat valley floor. I remember that it had already started to thaw back at the mouth of the pass, and it really started to warm up the further we went down. There was some sort of bracken growing among the boulders: it swayed like seaweed in the tide. Above, on the valley slopes, we saw men with ploughs and horses turning black peaty furrows across the meadows, some stopping now and then to wipe the beads of sweat from their foreheads as they watched us pass. It was all too much for me, what with the change in temperature and I guess I just went out cold because that was the last thing I clocked until I woke up in a dark place with sunlight playing through chinks in the drystone wall. I was so stiff I could hardly move. Pilgrim World was snoring like a pig next to me on the dirt floor. I just about managed to roll over to him and blew hard in his ear to wake him up.

"No... no..." he mumbled in his sleep, "I can explain about the stones. Just give me a chance..."

"Stop your jabbering and wake up!" I said. "Tell me where we are."

"Is that you?" he asked. "I thought you'd gone over the edge.... Oh, no, now I remember... it was you who threw my stones away!"

"Shut up about your stupid bloody stones and tell me where we are!"

"How long did I sleep?" He sounded stressed out and his lips were trembling. I felt kind of sorry for him.

"Two weeks," I said just to wind him up; actually I had no idea. "And you've only been raving away in your sleep the whole time too!"

"Oh, no! What did I say?"

"Too much by far, sonny. Is it true about Saffron Tinker?"

"I don't know what you're on about," he sulked. "Where are we?"

"You're supposed to tell me."

"I'm supposed to tell you what?"

"Jesus wept, Pilgrim!" I shouted, beginning to lose my rag. "I want to know where we are and what we're doing here and only you know the answer 'cos you're the only one who's been here before. Am I right? Now come on, spill the beans, is this Small Country?"

With a creak the door opened and a man's shadow fell across the threshold. He must have seen that we were awake because he slammed the door shut again and we could hear his footsteps tinkling like a piano as he sped away over the loose slates.

Soon the door opened again and six men's heads looked in against the light, their features obscured.

"Out," said one.

"I can't move," said poor Pilgrim but with that a lance from somewhere came and stabbed him in his arse. He moved pretty smartish then, and I followed sharply.

"This way," said the man.

Outside, the dazzling sunlight shone like shillings in our eyes and bounced from the leaves of the trees and danced in the streams and pools. Once I could see I laughed at Pilgrim World with his face as black as a collier and he laughed and said I looked just the same. We asked if they had any water we could wash with.

"No," answered the guard.

"You're welcome to water from my spring," said a pretty little maiden who'd appeared from somewhere and was standing in our path.

"Hurry up then," snarled the guard.

We made the most of our wash too as she poured spring water from her pitcher. With the cold cold water on our faces and a warm sun on our backs we quite soon felt a whole lot better.

"Aren't they friendly round here?" said Pilgrim once we had set off again.

There were all kinds of birds flitting about between the trees, types I'd never seen the likes of before on any nature programme back home in Lowland. Big clumsy birds with long golden tail feathers and black wings and red crests on their heads, calling and whistling to one another like referees and flocking to the bushes around us to get a good look and to see where we were going. The path slabs were worn smooth and being wet, flowed before us like quicksilver between the two high walls down towards a village of grey stone and slate with smoke rising like ribbons from the chimneys. Here the streets were paved with cobbles worn to a smooth glow, nice and gentle under foot. One house was larger than the rest, with the Small Country banner flying proudly from its pole on the roof. It was towards this house that they were taking us. In fact it was not a house but a hall. There were no holes in these walls, only fine plaster and murals of battle scenes and victories. Here were the Heartless Bodies defeated by Small Country warriors with white banners streaming. Over there the Wire Bandits on Shining Beasts flew from Small Country forces, with some of them planting the white star on a white ground above the battlefield. They seemed glad to have beaten the enemy rather than getting killed. I spent ages studying that white star on a white background trying to make out the star but I never found it.

"Grind Underfoot: Prince of Small Country," barked a cross little man from his raised throne. "I want answers and I want the truth. Do you two understand?"

"What's the question, sir?" asked Pilgrim and for his trouble got another spear stab off one of the soldiers.

"We will be pleased to co-operate in any way we can, Grind Underfoot, sir," I said. Grind Underfoot reached for a roll of parchment which he unrolled with a flourish.

"Where is Saffron Tinker?" was his first question.

"With the Bandits, sir," said Pilgrim.

"Of his own accord or against his will?"

"They didn't offer him any choice, sir, if that's what you mean," I replied. "But there's no way around it, he did kill that beast and..."

"Just look here!" growled Grind Underfoot, losing his temper. "I don't give a brass farthing who killed the beast. Saffron Tinker is supposed to be here so he can accompany you to the Lower Level! I can't send you without him!"

"It doesn't look as though we'll be going, then," I said.

He totally lost it then and started shouting. "You're damn lucky that Saffron Tinker's name is on the same draft paper as yours, boy! Otherwise I would derive the greatest pleasure in having

20

Giant Hands tear you limb from limb with his ten fine fingers!"

"Sorry, sir," I tried to appease him. "Of course we'll be going to the Lower Level.... When will Saffron Tinker be arriving?"

"Fool! Moron! Both of you are complete idiots! You're the ones who lost him and you have got to get him back again. There is nothing further to discuss! And just thinking about what will happen to you should you dare to fail makes even my bitter old blood curdle in my veins. Take them away!"

"I think he wants us to rescue Saffron Tinker," I said to Pilgrim World once we were alone, thankfully this time in a decent hut by the side of the hall.

"Is that it?" he said. "Do you think we'll manage?"

"No." I was telling him the truth for once.

"What if we refuse?"

"Don't even think about it. We've got three days to prepare."

You could say we made the most of it in New Village. Turns out that was where we were. There are other villages in Red County and other counties in Central Province, but this was the best one, according to the locals. We stayed put in New Village anyway, else I bet we'd only have got lost.

Right enough place, too, except for the electricity supply, long since disconnected and stolen by the Wire Bandits for sale to the Exile States. Since there was no electricity, the network screens were of no use either so the news came with old fashioned messengers, like postmen in the olden days. They made it from Small Country to Sunless Summer in less than a week, so they said, not like us pitching camp on the edge of the world and getting lost in Bleak Winter.

We were allowed to come and go as we pleased: all we had to do was say that we were working for Grind Underfoot and all doors would open before us, with people scrambling for us to accept their gifts.

Pilgrim World was delighted, of course, and went off to the storehouse to choose all manner of trinkets, and to scour the streams for colourful stones. I left him to it and went for a walk above the village.

I was quite happy looking at the birds looking at me, and whistling at them as they screeched crossly back at me for imitating them.

"Don't frighten the Flame Birds," said the little maiden, having appeared from nowhere with her pitcher of spring water on her head.

"Gosh," I said, startled, "you're a quiet one."

"You're from Lowland aren't you?" she asked. "Aren't you Gwern?"

"I am, yes," I said. "How d'you know?"

"I'm Summer Willow the water girl. How long are you staying in Small Country?"

"Three days. We're going to rescue Saffron Tinker," I boasted. "Tell me," I added, "haven't you got family in my town?"

"Down in Lowland? Oh, sure, my cousin Scarlet Nightshade. Know her? We moved to Small Country when the Heartless Bodies took my father and brother when I was small. I don't hear from my family back home often now. I try to write but it's not the same since we lost the Wire Post. The new messengers are so slow, aren't they?"

"I remember you leaving town. Weren't you about six or seven? Suppose I wasn't much older myself come to think of it."

"I'm late with Grind Underfoot's water," she said, smiling like the morning sun. "Maybe I'll see you around sometime."

I lingered awhile longer. I sat with my back to the earth bank by the spring listening to the water arching into the pool and watching the Flame Birds circling above me, whistling and winking at me and hopping from bough to bough in the branches.

Pilgrim was slumped lazily on his mattress when I got back. Worn out, he said, from choosing weapons for the journey back to Wild Country.

"I've been for a walk above the village, watching the Flame Birds," I told him. "Come on, it's time we went to look for some supper."

We went to Leather Belly's place for supper and ordered two bottles of bilberry spirits and roast meat with roast potatoes and a loaf of bread, putting it all down on Grind Underfoot's account.

"You'd better come with me tomorrow to get your weapons," said Pilgrim World as we ate. "There's a lot of choosing to be done, you know."

But I didn't go with Pilgrim World to choose weapons next day. I went for a walk above the village to see the Flame Birds going through their paces.

"Hia, Gwern," said Summer Willow over her shoulder as she bent over the spring pool to fill her pitcher. She never wears shoes and she had her skirts all hitched up around her waist with her naked legs glistening wet in the sunlight.

"It's a lovely day, Summer Willow," I said. "These birds are quite something, aren't they? Would you like a drop of bilberry spirits?" And I fished out the bottle that I'd kept from the night before and uncorked it.

She came to sit beside me by the bank and that's where we were drinking bilberry spirits and chatting about Lowland and Small Country and about everything under the sun. Then I put my arm around her waist and felt her warm and soft under her shirt. She rested her head on my shoulder as if she was terribly tired.

"You're so pretty, Summer Willow," I said in her ear as I bent to kiss her. Her lips were warm and yielding and her fragrance of blossoms filled my head but as the sun caressed my nape, and the green grass under us soothed us and I closed my eyes and enveloped myself in her warmth, my mind opened towards you and as we lay together I could hear the whirling of the warm insects and could see before me the emerald grass choking the path to Helen's Stone as swallows darted overhead and I could see the dry moss on the river stones. The river was only a bright trickle like water snaking down a plug hole and I could feel the sun's heat baking the stones of the orchard walls and see a dragonfly zig zagging on his whirling wings like a helicopter. You were hanging out sheets to dry in the garden, with the boy at your feet playing with the pegs. He pointed at me and made a gurgling noise in his throat and you turned to look as I walked up the path.

"You shouldn't have come," you said. "They'll know that you've been. Hey, Calonnog! Spit that out this minute!"

"I miss you Caress..."

"You can't miss something you've never had."

"Will you give me a bit of your heart to take with me? It would shelter me from the storm where I have to be. It's not much to ask of you..."

"You could have had my whole heart, Gwern, but now I know you'd only spoil it. The wound is only beginning to heal from the last time; things are different now. My heart belongs to the boy now, Gwern. You know that, don't you, and I'm sorry I can't give you my all any more."

I felt the world getting colder and I raised my head and heard the arched water plunge hard into the spring pool and saw a little cloud swallow the sun as Summer Willow opened her eyes and raised her head to see. A sharp breeze was blowing, the Flame Birds had long since vanished from the trees and the evening dew was deep and menacing on the bowed blades of the green grass.

"Damn that cloud," she said nestling closer.

A long time passed and the ground grew cold.

"Best not to mention I've been up here with you, drinking and so on...." I said but I couldn't keep my voice from grating.

"Why then?" she said looking puzzled.

"Listen, Summer Willow, just in case you've got the wrong idea, I only came up here to keep you company; it must be lonely up here drawing water by yourself all day. The spirits went straight to my head...."

All she did was jump angrily to her feet, straighten her skirts, snatch her pitcher and stride away from me with her bare feet slapping like flatfish on the smooth stones.

I felt quite down-hearted as I went back to our lodgings and there I sat for ages at the table by the window with my head on my arms until Pilgrim World came in looking very worried.

"Who's eaten your porridge this time, then?" I asked sharply.

"You never came with me to choose your weapons for tomorrow," he answered. "Come on, hurry up, we'd better go now."

I decided to go with him anyhow, anything to turn my thoughts away from what you'd be thinking about me now.

They could only offer us old fashioned weapons, Pilgrim World told me. Obviously he now knew all there was to know about them all, having spent his three days selecting them. The new ones were useless, apparently, because there was no energy left to power them. But had there been, believe me, that would have been some hot gear! Hand to air missiles still gleaming in their paper, electric distortion bullets in their clean cotton wool covers, desiccation rays, all you could imagine. And Pilgrim still badgering me, "Look, that's a good one, Gwern, and here, look, come on look at this one, isn't that a fantastic machine if it would only work." I saw restplates by the dozen, hard and transparent like that one Dave Egg Stealer lent me, every size to fit like a glove; three edged swords, tridents, crossbows all worthy of some museum. They kept them in the town lockup, a dreadful place. Six of the Swarthy Cavedwarves, smaller even than Grind Underfoot, had come from the caves of Bleak Winter to work as warders of the prison. Two prisoners: two Heartless Bodies, chained fast in a dark hole. Each of the Cavedwarves would be obliged to thump both prisoners six times a day and thrice at night, so it was no surprise that they both looked the worse for wear. We went to their cell for a chat between wallops.

Very chatty they were too, the Heartless Bodies. They're on the side of the Exile Sates, that's what Saffron Tinker'd told us. Many of them aren't even from the Exile States but by the time Rausman and his Counsellors have finished brainwashing them and their hearts have been taken away, they follow orders and fight where they are told. I'm sure I'd have been made a Heartless Body had Fischermädchen caught me and handed me over to Rausman's Counsellors. And the only treatment for Heartless Bodies in Small Country is to beat them, because without electricity the head wires are no use at all, and the beatings seem to calm them down. These two were actually volunteers from Zigenner City in the southern Exile States. They were full of praise for how they'd been treated, saying how lucky they were to have survived the carnage in Bleak Winter the last time they'd tried to crush Small Country. Turned out of course they hadn't actually survived, but'd been brought back to life by the Swarthy Cavedwarves' healing herbs so as to be sold for a unit a head to Grind Underfoot. Of course this little system kept the lockup Cavedwarves in work as well.

"Actually it's been quite super," said the bald one called Wasser Schwoll. "They've all been frightfully hospitable."

"Isn't it a drag getting beaten black and blue all the time?" I asked, feigning interest in their affairs.

"Certainly not!" said the one called Herz Erklingt with his matted grey hair wrapped about his body. "It's most essential to develop a physical relationship with one's captors. We feel privileged to receive such attention."

"What did he say?" asked Pilgrim.

"Time for your hiding," said the largest Cavedwarf.

"Just a minute," I cut across. "We're here on official business on behalf of Grind Underfoot, so shut your gob and go make us some tea."

He went, too. The tea was like piss although the two without hearts enjoyed it. The dwarf had even found some biscuits.

We learnt a lot from these poor hostages. They were surprised that I spoke their language so well.

"What I don't understand," I said, "is why the Wire Bandits would steal Small Country's power supply. I thought they were part of the confederation together with Lowland and all the rest under the presidency of Small Country. Surely they would be wiser not to break ranks like this but stand firm together to prevent the Exile States taking back our freedom? They'll get nowhere at each other's throats like this."

"But of course, old man," said Herz Erklingt. "Quite inexplicable, we don't pretend to understand. Together you would be unconquerable. However I firmly believe that war is now inevitable, as naturally the Exile States are bound to take a dim view of your unilateral declaration of independence. They were not even consulted about the matter. I am convinced that in this instance the whole edifice of this paltry alliance shall crumble before our superior tactical organisation. This time it will be final. *Zurüchschlagen*!"

"*Zugang Zurüchschlagen*!" rejoined the bald one. They were starting to get excited and trying to get up from the floor but the fetters kept them down.

"Shut your filthy mouths," shouted one of the warders. I held up my hand and spoke in his ear promising him another unit if he'd give them both an extra beating that evening. We bade farewell and were soon back at our lodgings by the hall in the centre of New Village.

We were supposed to set out the following morning. And set out we did. I'd chosen a restplate and some other junk for the journey, together with a tent and a mule. Pilgrim, of course, had selected a pile of weapons high as a mountain, a sackful of stones and a herd of mules to carry all his kit. "Fool," I thought, seeing him struggle with all his things for a futile journey.

Down in Bleak Winter the weather hit us like a sledge-hammer. I was having trouble enough with Pilgrim World and his obstreperous mules. The packs were always falling off and Pilgrim would be tying them back on again every two minutes. The mules would then just stop pointblank or once they'd get going, they wouldn't stop; anything to drive Pilgrim crazy and to hold up our journey.

I wasn't exactly surprised when the Swarthy Cavedwarves fell upon us and stole ten of Pilgrim's mules, leaving him crying like a baby in a wet nappy.

"Hush now," I tried to soothe him. "You've still got six left, and look, I've only got one. So really, what are you crying about?"

"Yes, but you only had one to start with," he whimpered, "and I had sixteen fine mules and now I've only got six. That's really not fair, I'm so cut up about it." And he started blubbering again.

"I bet the mules aren't gutted over losing you," I said, beginning to lose patience.

"Fish get gutted, not mules!" he snapped back.

I was about to cuff him sharply on the ear when the Ice Locusts descended upon us. A lucky intervention for Pilgrim.

They were rising up over the edge of the precipice and raining down hard upon us like hailstones. The mules were struggling and Pilgrim World started wailing all the louder and there was I damning and cursing and trying to kill the Ice Locusts with a two yard sword.

When we were on all fours, pinned to the ground by the swarm, the Swarthy Cavedwarves returned to plunder us again.

"Enough," commanded Snow Storm leader of the Cavedwarves, and the locusts rose from us at once.

"Throw them over the precipice," she instructed her followers, who grabbed us, inching us towards the edge.

"You're making a mistake!" I cried.

"Not at all," she said. "This is the precipice we always use."

"We have messages for you from the Small Country Jailhouse Cavedwarves," I shouted from the edge.

"Drop them," said Snow Storm.

"On the ground, she means," screamed Pilgrim, struggling as they lowered him over the edge of the abyss.

We were treated to a fine welcome after all that, though. They started to look on us as proper gentlefolk, allowing us to visit their caves, meet their families and warm ourselves on Ice Locust stew.

We told them that the Jailhouse Cavedwarves sent their regards and that the heartless pair was still being beaten and that there was talk there might be many more Heartless Bodies available in Bleak Winter soon who could be sold for a good price as hostages to Grind Underfoot. Snow Storm and her husband Rustrat were delighted to hear the news and they didn't even bother to take all our mules, nor even all our weapons, as they had threatened, but let us keep a mule each. They also packed up plenty of Ice Locust sandwiches for our journey and a bag of healing herbs into the bargain.

"Look us up any time," they called as we rode away.

"Certainly," called back Pilgrim. "When we can afford it," he added dryly.

"You're very materialistic for someone who calls himself Pilgrim," I chided him as we left their sight.

"What does that mean?"

"Getting off on possessions and weapons and mules and such like."

"Well I never had any before and anyway I like animals, so what's wrong with that?"

"Oh, nothing, forget it," I muttered, turning away and ignoring him from then on.

The Ice Locusts didn't bother us after that and we managed to reach Wild Country by nightfall without further trouble. There was our tent, as we'd left it, in the middle of the camp ledge on the mountain escarpment. The body of the Shining Beast was still there too, under its pile of stones, but we didn't approach it that evening. The rocky peaks rose up like islands in a sea of cotton wool, with the setting sun dyeing it pink. The clouds seemed so solid, you'd expect them to hold you easily if you jumped onto them from the icy brink. We pitched a few stones down from the ledge to test the theory but they always seemed to disappear before reaching the clouds. Night fell around us and we went back to the tent. It was quiet as the grave, no lowing of Shining Beasts to frighten us in the darkness, only the growing sound of Pilgrim's breathing and of the canvas whispering until I couldn't sleep for all the noise in my head. It was lucky I still had my restplate.

The next morning we went to take a look at the Shining Beast's grave. We dragged a few stones from around his head to see how he was. He was much the same as before, dead. The cold, though (and his precious "special stones") had kept him in a decent state; well, apart from the maggots in his wounds.

"Will the healing herbs bring him back to life again?" asked Pilgrim.

"I doubt it," I said. "But we might as well try, I suppose."

So we built a fire to thaw some ice from the mountain and boiled it up to make tea with the healing herbs. Then we took all the stones off the Shining Beast and packed the tea leaves into his wounds, pouring some of the tea down his throat and rubbing him with more healing herbs. By then it was time for lunch.

We had our lunch in the tent: Ice Locust sandwiches, the ones the Swarthy Cavedwarves had kindly given us in return for the roast geese and spiced sausages that we'd brought with us for the journey. Foul tasting things Ice Locusts are too; not much nutrition in them either, if the appearance of the Swarthy Cavedwarves is anything to go by.

We were busy trying to force down the last of these sandwiches when we heard a weak voice calling "Bwwwwww" so we got up and went out to have a look.

The Shining Beast had risen shakily to his feet and was looking around him. The hide had healed all along his flank, apart from a little claw-shaped scar on his shoulder where the weapon had gone in. He was awfully thin, though, with all his ribs showing through his skin.

"Hurray!" shouted Pilgrim. "The special stones have done the trick!"

"Hold the champagne, nitwit," I reproached him, "and go boil up a saucepan of porridge for him, quick as you can."

"None left," he said. "Only Ice Locust sandwiches."

The Shining Beast guzzled the few sandwiches we had left and was still hungry so I sent off Pilgrim World to look for moss and grass and stuff. He came back in the end with a huge armful of rushes and moss which the beast was soon munching noisily. By the following morning he was right as rain: we were the ones who were starving now.

"What's for breakfast?" asked Pilgrim World as soon as he woke up.

"Nothing."

"Has the Shining Beast eaten all we've got?"

"'Course he has. And here you are wasting all your energy dragging a sack of stones around with you everywhere, you'll drive me mad!" I grabbed at his sack. "What else have you got in here?"

"Get off! Let go...." But I was stronger than Pilgrim World and I prised the sack off him and emptied it onto the floor of the tent. And what do you think he'd got under the stones? Tins of baked beans, tins of sardines, packets of pancakes, jam, butter, slabs of chocolate... and two roast geese.

"Well for Christ's sake, you selfish little pig," I cried, losing it big time. "Hiding all this food from me and stuffing yourself behind my back! And all the while pretending to be starving! I'll throw you over the edge myself, you greedy swine!" I wouldn't really have done it but it was enough to frighten him.

"But I really am starving. I haven't eaten anything from the sack, honestly. I'm disciplining myself to overcome temptation, that's all.... Can I put the food back now?"

"What utter rubbish! Overcoming temptation? If you don't pass me the tin opener right now, the temptation to stone you to death with your own 'special' stones will be too much for me to bear and I won't even try to resist it!"

A hearty breakfast later we were both feeling a lot better. There's just no end to that silly Pilgrim's antics, I tell you straight.

We set off again soon after, the two of us riding the Shining Beast and the mules tethered behind. The tent we left where it was, now that we had a spare one. We gave the beast free rein to take us wherever he wanted in the hope that he might sniff out an old trail that would lead us to Switchback City, but unfortunately he didn't.

One good thing about Pilgrim World is his sharp eyesight. He can spot a pin head at a hundred yards and tell whether it's rusty or not. Of course he would miss the most obvious thing right under his nose, but that's beside the point: he spotted the pylons. He pointed out a long line of them marching over the hills far below us, while I saw nothing. The Shining Beast refused to take us that way so we brought the mules up from behind and tied the beast by two long ropes to the mules' collars, mounted them and led him like that. The bull beast could have dragged us to kingdom come had he so desired, being four times the size of both mules together, but he chose to be led as docile as a pet lamb. And there was no trouble getting the mules to move it with a huge Shining Beast breathing down their necks, all the way from the rough rocky regions to a boundless marshy plain where cotton grass was bowing in the wind. Over where the pylon lines dipped behind a distant knoll we could see red and yellow lights flickering and tinting the low clouds. We approached warily in case anyone should see us coming, but there was no one there. The lines between two pylons had been uncoupled and a heavy black cable had been connected, which dangled down, sparking furiously with a sound like frying fat.

"This is the work of the Wire Bandits," said Pilgrim.

"However did you work that out," I replied.

We followed the cable as it wound like a huge black eel between the marshes and the knolls. It was only as it got dark that we made out the lights of Switchback City in the distance. At first all we noticed was a glow reflected in the clouds and then we saw it, spread out on the horizon like a shower of stars fallen to earth.

The Shining Beast was getting restless, probably sensing that the herd was close. We could hear their lowing in the distance; at least they didn't seem up to making the sort of din they liked to make back on the escarpment. Sam, our beast, was completely better by now. Hearing the herd he puffed himself up to his full height, easily three yards to his shoulder, and raised up his massive bull-like head to blow hot air into the sky and flash his electric eyes. He was always docile with us though, thank God, and would insist on sleeping with his head sticking into our tent.

We decided to pitch camp on the marshland that night, in case we lost him in the darkness. All around us we could hear nothing but the sound of the Shining Beasts lowing and snorting and chewing the cud, and their pungent smell was heavy on the cold air.

"I'll never get to sleep here," moaned Pilgrim.

"A good job too," I replied. "Someone has to stand guard in case Sam tries to do a runner."

"You won't try to escape from Pilgrim, will you Sam?" cooed Pilgrim.

"Bwwwwwww," said Sam.

The next morning Pilgrim World was snoring like a hog and Sam was gone. I gave him a kick in the ear and he screamed.

"I'll kill you for this you useless scarecrow," I shouted at him.

"He's probably just outside," said Pilgrim, rubbing his ear.

We went out to look. There was nothing but a sea of Shining Beasts peacefully grazing all around us and each of them just like the next. It's only when they get cross they start to flash their electric eyes so we were Ok for the time being. But if I'd had electric eyes at that moment I'd have flashed them at Pilgrim World and burnt him to a cinder.

Our mules had also buggered off with Sam during the night. We were ravenous and weak as two rag dolls. We couldn't even take down the tent, but stumbled on towards Switchback City. We were such a sight that no one took any notice of us.

Switchback City is a wild place. It's not a proper city, more like a shanty town of corrugated iron huts with tangled cobwebs of wires in every direction. All over the place the wires spark and smoulder and crackle like one of Betsan's fry-ups.

"Excuse me, but we're looking for Rock Jaw," Pilgrim World asked of a wild looking harridan who was busy plucking a duck in the doorway of her cabin.

"AAAAAaaaaargh!" she screamed at the top of her voice, letting the duck fall from her grasp. The duck scrambled frantically away from her, quacking loudly, the woman all shouts and menacing pointing fingers. I suppose the locals weren't used to seeing strangers. In no time at all we were brought before Rock Jaw who eyed us suspiciously.

"We brought the Shining Beast, sir," I croaked.

"Get up off that floor you moron," he said, giving me a kick up the backside which sent me half a yard into the air. "Where is he then?"

"I'm afraid he got free last night, sir," I answered. "Pilgrim World here was supposed to guard him but he fell asleep. Off he went with our two mules. He must be with his friends in the middle of the herd by now."

"Do you think I'm going to buy that one?" said Rock Jaw, reaching for a meat cleaver and starting to trim a bit around his beard. "I have ten thousand Shining Beasts out there."

"You've got ten thousand and one now," said Pilgrim, bless him.

"Take the comedian for a walk, Blue Gash," said Rock Jaw with a yawn. "You might like to show him your spear collection?"

We could hear Pilgrim's screams for ages after.

"Isn't he a silly fool," I said. "It's all his fault. But I'll find your beast for you, Rock Jaw, honest I will. Can Saffron Tinker be set free afterwards?"

"No he can not. And neither can you. I'm annoyed. I'm angry. Nothing's going right at the moment. And with Burnt Tongue nagging me all the time…. Debts coming out of my ears and scores to settle, too. At least I'll get a few minutes break this afternoon when it's time to feed the ravenous beasts. Your mate is a bit on the skinny side, but no matter. Granite Fist and Chews Boulders, take him away."

"I'm so sorry to hear things aren't going too well, sir," I called as they dragged me out by the feet. "Really," I muttered out loud, "I don't know what's so bloody special about that beast."

"It's curtains for you, anyway, sonny," said one of the guards, having overheard me. "Losing Rock Jaw's bull beast! Ho, ho, ho…." I couldn't have amused them more had I been a circus clown.

"Well what was the work of that bull beast then? What's Saffron Tinker been forced to do?"

"Ha, ha, ha… you'll find out soon enough. Saffron Tinker's on his last legs by now, I expect. He will be glad of your help, I'm sure. Here we are, open up the cage, Chews Boulders, in he goes!"

God, Saffron Tinker looked tired. He hardly raised an eyebrow in my direction as I sailed into the cell. His beard was matted and his purple nose was dull. The Shining Beasts must be a pretty criminal lot as well, I thought, as there was a cell full of them there too, stinking worse than Saffron Tinker.

"Long time, no see, Saffron Tinker," I said in case he didn't recognise me.

"Not tonight," replied the poor fellow, really out of it.

"It's me, Gwern Excuses!"

"Can't you see the red cross on their sides?"

"No, listen, it's Gwern Excuses, come to rescue you, Tinker. That beast you killed is right as rain again."

"Yes, sir, all these ones already seen to. Look at the crosses!"

"Don't you understand, Saffron Tinker! Pilgrim World is around here somewhere too. We'll all get out of here, you'll see!"

"It is crucial."

"Yes, Tinker, yes it is."

"Sir, it is crucial that I be accorded a ladder boasting a view over the newspaper with November externally at its base if you would be so kind or I shall telephone for additional eggs."

"I don't know," I said, unable to make head nor tail of his gibberish. "Anyway, we lost the bull Shining Beast on the way so who knows when we'll get out of here now."

"Oh you irresponsible rascals!" Saffron Tinker raised two tired eyelids revealing angry yellow eyes. "I'll kill you both! Where is Pilgrim?"

"He was rude to Rock Jaw. He has a good shouting voice, hasn't he?"

"*Had*, I'm afraid. Poor thing. A pity. Rest in Peace etcetera. What is the time? Oh, yes, there they are, by now I would imagine."

"Stop rambling and speak straight, man!"

"Yes, wormwood and a half in a bucket is what I said and no treacle on it this time, thanking you very much too, you unkempt old magpie!"

"Pull yourself together, Tinker!"

"And how does the husband like prison then? Better off there, by all acounts, than being with you, you dirty sow not even bothering to wash the sheets before eating them and I know all about your gorging yourself while I starved, you swollen suet pudding, to hell with you, spending all my few savings on your chapel hats and funeral handkerchiefs, you swollen stinkhorn stripping the trees of their leaves in Winter and strutting around as if you were related to Snowdon, but you will be disappointed! I will silence you, oh yes... oh yes I will, I will..."

"Let go of me, you crazy madman," I shouted as he tried to

36

strangle me, thinking that I was Mrs Tinker, come back to haunt him after he did her in one drunken night without telling anybody because he'd had enough. Pilgrim World knew the full story and he'd let slip enough of it talking in his sleep on the back of his mule in Bleak Winter.

Thank heavens there were plenty of loose rocks strewn around on the cell floor and I got hold of a heavy one and let him have it on the temple until I could see little stars circling around his head. His grip slackened and he crumbled to the floor like a sandcastle, lying there groaning and dribbling blood and blathering quietly to himself. I stepped back and went to sit in the farthest corner of the cage to think things over.

"Oh, what the hell will I do now?" I said to myself. "Where is that serpent Pilgrim; gone and left me? Tinker's lost his marbles and I'll lose mine here.... Oh, what shall I do? Why did they have to come for me at all? There's worse ones than me who've been allowed to stay and no one persecutes them.... It was that bitch Scarlet Nightshade who started all this, does she think I don't know she's thick as thieves with Fischermädchen? It was her told Fischermädchen who'd programmed the virus into the Persuasion Department's computer software.... And now this...."

My poor head felt brittle as a robin's egg, the cage was undulating like the waves of the sea before my eyes and the Shining Beasts were nudging their damp noses into my face, blackness was closing around me and there I was in broad daylight, standing once again on the cart track to Helen's Stone where the leaves fell in showers and the bracken rusted, where the bowed grass was wet underfoot and the slabbed path slippery as soap, where the crows cawed from the crowns of the stark oaks and the smell of the far marshes hung upon the breeze. I walked on as the river dressed its white ribbons about the rocks, while the cobwebs of drizzle clung to my hair and the flattened smoke slunk from the chimney and I knocked and heard your voice calling "Come in". I went in to the warm smell of a wood fire and ironing clothes and you put down the iron and glared at me with pin-prick pupils.

"What do you want?"

"I came to see you and Calonnog."

"He's not here. You've got a nerve. Coming here bold as brass when everyone knows what you've been up to. Get out of here, go on back to your Summer Willow, and all the others too, you two-timing scumbag!"

"Where is he?"

"With Scarlet Nightshade. You won't see him again. Get out of my sight. I don't want you here."

"Let me explain..."

"Come one step closer and you'll get this iron in your face. Just go!"

"You watch your back with that Scarlet Nightshade. Be careful, Caress. One day you'll know who to trust."

"Get out, you two-faced bastard! And don't show your face here ever again!" With that you started to shake me like a rattle, shoving me back towards the door until I was reeling from side to side and you were hitting me about the head with the iron as I bent like a reed in the wind on the moors and the whole room darkened, spinning away from me at the end of a long tunnel like looking down the wrong end of a telescope and Pilgrim's voice called, "Wake up, Gwern, wake up will you?" as he stood over me shaking me like a rag doll and whacking me about the head with his shoe.

"What the hell d'you want?" I said peevishly. "Can't you see I'm sleeping, leave me alone."

"Snap out of it, Gwern, hurry up! We're leaving!"

"How did you get here, Pilgrim?" I spluttered as I came to my senses. "I thought you'd been fed to the beasts for cheeking Rock Jaw?"

"Oh, that? Yes," he said as if he was well used to it by now, "but I found Sam so Rock Jaw says we can go now."

"Where did you find him, Pilgrim?"

"It was him who found me, actually," he said, scratching his nose dreamily. "There I was, lying at the bottom of Rock Jaw's ditch, and Granite Fist was letting the ravenous beasts out of the fasting pen, ready to eat me up when along comes a massive Shining Beast from behind him and topples him into the ditch on top of me. Then the beast bends his big black head down to me until I grab his horns and he pulls me out and starts licking my face and blowing warm air like the smell of biscuits up my nose while the ravenous beasts swallow up Granite Fist. There was a little scar the shape of a claw on his shoulder and I shouted, 'Sam!' And that's how I got pardoned for being cheeky to Rock Jaw, although I never really meant to be cheeky at all, it's just he's thin-skinned as a frog and…"

"Yes, yes, very good, you can shut up now," I interrupted. "Where's Saffron Tinker?"

"With the mules."

"Oh dear," I said, my mood heading downwards. "Thinks he's a mule now, does he?"

"Not really. Actually he thinks he's a saddle and wants to be stretched over his mule's back with his hands and feet making a girth under the mule's belly just like the Wire Bandits tied him before, and he wants me to sit on top of him."

"Well, at least we won't have any trouble getting him back if he stays like that."

Boulder Biter held the door open as we left the cage. "I'm sorry about Granite Fist," I said to him as I passed.

"I'm not," he replied.

"It's not my usual style to thank anyone for anything," said Rock Jaw as we stood before him in the Big Hut. "So bugger off before you get on my nerves. But before you go, is there anything you'd like to take with you as a souvenir?"

"I'd be very happy if I could keep these little stones I collected in your ditch," said Pilgrim.

"Keep them then, and treasure them," said Rock Jaw. "Saffron Tinker, what do you choose?"

"I'll have my girths oiled with goose fat so that the leather may be supple, should you see her say I must remember to append a foreword."

"Boulder Biter!" shouted Rock Jaw. "Smite the lunatic." Boulder Biter boxed Saffron Tinker's ears and the Tinker thanked him heartily.

"Gwern Excuses," Rock Jaw turned regally towards me. "What would you like as your souvenir of Switchback City?"

"Well, sir, since you're so generous as to offer, I was wondering would it be possible for you to restore the electricity supply to Small Country please? It's so boring there without television, sir."

"Fine," said Rock Jaw. "And now, adieu to the three of you. Give my regards to Grind Underfoot... Oh, and tell him that the wires predict war."

"Of course we will, sir," said Pilgrim World and out we went to the mules. Pilgrim adjusted Saffron Tinker on the mule's back and then climbed up on him as we set out for Small Country without once looking back in case Rock Jaw changed his mind.

Testimony Three

I recall that our journey back to Small Country was as long, cold and miserable as ever but that's about it, I'm afraid, since Saffron Tinker ate the energy pack of my mobile processor so I couldn't make notes.

We obviously made it to Small Country, and got a hero's welcome to boot. Small Country's White Star banners all out along the streets, and crowds on their doorsteps cheering us on, others waving at us from upstairs windows and throwing all colour of paper streamers overhead as we passed. High in the air the Flame Birds were throwing their own colourful circles and screeching at us like head-cases. All this and the meowing of the pipers and the booming of the drums, with the sun beating down, all this sent my head spinning faster than Wil Pickled Herring's head on a Sunday morning.

Of course Pilgrim World was lapping it up. You'd think the fun and games had all been laid on special for him, the way he rode on Saffron Tinker through the crush, smiling like a Cheshire Cat and waving in triumph. Every now and then he'd rise up in his stirrups to count how many had turned out and cursing that no one had bothered to lay palm leaves before his mule. Saffron Tinker underneath him had managed to get one hand free from his thongs and was shaking his fist, swearing and shouting some drivelling twaddle as he tried to raise his head to gob on anyone within spitting distance.

What with these two acting up like this and the crowd pressing in on us and the mules forever stopping to graze the coloured streamers, no wonder we took a good hour to reach Grind Underfoot's hall, and no wonder at all that he was in a foul mood because no one keeps Grind Underfoot waiting.

"Where the hell have you been?" was all the welcome we had from him.

"We've been to Wild Country where we rescued Saffron Tinker from the Wire Bandits," said Pilgrim, grinning to split his mug.

"Come here," commanded Grind Underfoot. Up Pilgrim World went to the throne. "Bend forward," said he and without another word Grind Underfoot lashed out a ringing blow to his forehead. "Stupid boy," he added with another stinging clout to the side of his head. "I happen to have been waiting for you here for one hour and ten minutes. Nobody slights Grind Underfoot in this way without paying penance for an offence against a prince." With that he brought his knee up between Pilgrim's legs, making him close up like a book and collapse into a groaning heap on the floor. "Do you understand now, you insolent little weevil?"

"YYyyyesss, sir... yyyyess, sir..." whimpered Pilgrim, his smile wiped like chalk from a blackboard, "I'm very sorry, sir... It won't happen again, sir."

"That's better," said Grind Underfoot. "Now get up off my floor, you maggot or you'll spoil the shine on my slates. Get back to those two other monkeys down there!" Pilgrim had hardly struggled to his feet when he was dealt a mighty kick in the arse which sent him sailing through the air to land on his nose at our feet.

"Why is it always me that gets it?" whined Pilgrim World through his tears. I kicked him to make him shut up.

"Now then," continued Grind Underfoot, "here is an invoice each for the value of this insult to me. One hour ten minutes of a prince's time at ten thousand units an hour, that makes three thousand eight hundred and eighty units each to be paid within seven days. And now, finally, what tidings from Wild Country?"

I nudged Pilgrim World with my foot to get him to stand up and give his report. Clearing his throat with a cough, he announced: "Burnt Tongue, wife of Rock Jaw says there are no tidings at all now since the viruses corrupted her tidings terminal software. But I found some nice red stones in Grind Underfoot's ditch, sir, and he let me keep them as a souvenir of Switchback City, because it was me who found his Shining Beast, sir, and these are the very best stones that I ever had, sir, look, how they sparkle and shine."

"Bring them here... hmmm... these are mine now." It was heartbreaking to watch Pilgrim fight back the tears as he passed his precious little collection over to Grind Underfoot.

"Saffron Tinker is very quiet," announced Grind Underfoot, turning his attention away from Pilgrim. "Take that gag from his mouth and let us hear what he has to say."

"Begging your pardon, sir," I ventured, "but I'm not sure how wise that would be, sir..."

"Do it!" screamed Grind Underfoot and we tore the binding from Tinker's head and pulled the rag from his mouth.

"Saffron Tinker," declared Grind Underfoot, "present your report from Switchback City. Were you treated well?"

"Treated? I only got the treatment, that's all; what the hell's the matter with you all here, where's the goose fat I ordered, no one's lubricated the girth straps, the back-chain's loose from the pack-saddle and God alone knows where this scatterbrained boy's put the breeches-strap, he must be sorely punished for this, I'm telling you, and what's the use me telling you and nobody taking a blind bit of notice when I say the girth needs tightening and this one here riding as if he had his trousers full of ants it's no wonder his mule is unruly, good Lord Jesus he's a giddy goat, this boy, there's nothing in there between those two cabbage ears of his, I know from bitter experience, oh yes, many's the time I've been there searching for the breeches-strap and finding nothing but cobwebs and a dusty copy of *Pilgrim's Progress* with the pages all stuck together and the little rascal knows full well I can't stand the smell of that grease he rubs on his backside because he's such a pampered softy who isn't used to riding mules, always walking everywhere like some wingless heron, my God he needs some sense knocking into his head, so he does and if you won't do it then I will and I'm telling you..."

"That's enough!" shouted Grind Underfoot, blood pressue rising.

"Don't smarmy up to me just because you've lost the best saddle you ever had. You won't get me and that's that! Go to hell!"

"Put the rag back in his mouth!" roared Grind Underfoot, bouncing up and down with rage. "If I had permission I would torture him to death with a hot poker for that!"

"Why the hell do you need permission if you're a prince?" shouted Saffron Tinker, spitting out the rag we were trying to force into his mouth. "You're just a tin-pot princeling, having to get permission from Faithful Night, probably even has to ask to go to the toilet I surpoooooonngngngn ngngnwweengwee...." The rag did the trick eventually and we bound it tight.

"I'm afraid he's lost his marbles, sir," I apologised. "He was forced to live in a cage full of Shining Beasts, day in day out after he killed Sam, Rock Jaw's bull beast. You mustn't take any notice of him, sir."

"What about you, then, sonny boy?" said Grind Underfoot, still steaming like a kettle. "What's your story? Come on."

"Humbly report, sir, Rock Jaw sends his regards and has agreed to restore the electricity supply."

"That's done it! Right, I shall have you torn limb from limb for that! You're even madder than the other two! Sends me his regards, indeed! Restored the electricity supply, indeed! Oh, you disgusting little specimen, come here!"

"But it's true, sir, look, you'll see." I ran to the nearest light switch. Nothing happened.

"Guards, arrest him!" he shouted as I ran from switch to switch down the hall.

"Needs a new bulb, probably," Pilgrim suggested helpfully, "or perhaps a fuse has blown."

"Rock Jaw said something else as well," I called over my shoulder as I dodged the guards. "He said the wires predicted war and..." I couldn't finish because Giant Hands had got hold of me and was beginning to twist my head from my shoulders.

Grind Underfoot raised a hand and my head was released.

"Well why didn't you say so before? Guards, bring bulbs from the storeroom and get Serge Power to fix the fuse."

The bulbs were replaced. The fuse was mended. On went the switch and a wave of white light rippled from one end of the hall to the other like a stone thrown into a pool. Grind Underfoot switched on his network screen which hummed and whirred, flashing up the opening menu.

"You can go," said Grind Underfoot, not looking up from his screen. He seemed to have lost interest in us. "Oh, just a minute," he added. "The three of you are to present yourselves tonight in the Lower Level... And don't forget that you owe me for the insult!"

On our way out who should we meet but Summer Willow bringing spring water for Grind Underfoot.

"Hello, Summer Willow," I said looking down at my feet, blushing.

She strode right past us as if I wasn't even there.

"Know her, do you?" asked Pilgrim. "Wasn't that..."

"No, not really."

"Nggnggg wwwww ngg," said Saffron Tinker but we couldn't understand him with his mouth full of rags.

Outside on the street the flags had already been taken down and the coloured streamers swept away. The Flame Birds too had gone to roost and only an evening breeze stirred up the dust in the gutters. Hardly anyone was about and those that were kept their heads down as they went about their business, as if struggling against a strong wind.

We struck out sharply for the edge of town. On turning a corner we bumped into a little old lady bent almost double, dragging a heavy sack behind her.

"Excuse me," I asked, taking a step back, "do you know the way to the Lower Level?"

She didn't answer, didn't even raise her head; just struggled on past us without a word.

"Ngggannngw," said Saffron Tinker, pointing with his elbow towards the hills.

"This way," declared Pilgrim, crossing the road.

"The mad leading the blind," I said, following them out of the village into the blue and white moonlit night of the mountain.

Having spent several hours stumbling about the arid hillsides, we stumbled across a great oak door studded with iron nail heads like blackcurrants and with a massive oak frame at the foot of a sheer white granite cliff face which sparkled in the moonlight.

"This is where he lives, probably," said Pilgrim World wiping the sweat from his brow, the dry soil crunching under his boots as he turned towards it.

"Who d'you mean?" I asked.

"Well the Answer Keeper of course," and he knocked hard on the door.

No one came so he grabbed hold of the latch, pulled the door towards him on rasping hinges and stuck his head in.

"Ouch!" he cried, stepping back and holding his head in his hands.

"Silly fool," I said leaning forwards to rap my knuckles on the smooth white wall of granite that blocked the doorway.

We went on our way, clambering up the hillside and string me up if there wasn't a black hole, right there on the summit, with stone steps leading down into the bowels of the mountain.

"You see, I was right," said Pilgrim. "That's where he lives all right! Down there in the Lower Level!"

"Nggwaa nggwaaa," said Saffron Tinker, backing off. We hauled him after us like a mule with two ropes Pilgrim had in his sack.

"May as well see what we find," I said and down we went.

The Answer Keeper must be very stingy, I thought, or perhaps he doesn't realise that the power supply is back on. The black hole of Calcutta would be light as day compared with this hole, for Chrissake.

Reaching step number one thousand two hundred and something going down, Pilgrim made me lose count by asking the Answer Keeper's phone number.

"How the hell would I know?" I snapped angrily. "Why've you got to ask such stupid questions; you've made me lose count, you brainless gecko!"

"I just thought we could phone him to see if he's home."

"Christ Almighty!" I exclaimed, "I suppose you've got a mobile in that sack too, have you? It won't work down here, you know."

"No, no, Gwern, there's a phone in the wall here. I can feel it under my hand. Look..."

"Oh yeah, right, like I can just look," I said, feeling my way towards his voice, keeping my palm to the rough wall to try to find what he was on about.

It really was a phone though and as I put the receiver to my ear a voice said "Lower Level triple zero."

"Is the Answer Keeper home?" I asked.

"Who's there?" asked the voice.

"Us."

"Who are you?"

"Gwern Excuses, Pilgrim World and Mad Saffron Tinker."

"Come in."

"In where?"

"Put the phone down, then turn into the tunnel that will open before you to your right as you go down."

"Could you switch on the lights for us?" But the voice was gone.

The tunnel was as dark as the stone stairs but wider and as we followed it the walls fell away and soon our footsteps were echoing in space that seemed to reach in all directions around us. We turned this way and that in the dark, free to move without obstruction, apart from when we bumped into each other now and then. We heard Saffron Tinker let out a panicky "Nggwaaa Ngggwwaaaa" and stopped to listen for the echo of his voice from some far off wall, but the sound was gone like a stone falling into cloud.

"Welcome," the voice whispered by our side.

"Is that what you call it," snivelled Pilgrim; turns out he's afraid of the dark.

"Are you the Answer Keeper?" I asked.

The voice laughed heartily, "I am Faithful Night, my friends. His servant. It was I who ordered Grind Underfoot to send you here."

"How can a servant order a prince to do anything?" said Pilgrim who seemed to have got over his initial fright. Faithful Night took no notice of him.

"I have work for you," he said.

"Ngwaa Ngwaa Nggng," said Saffron Tinker.

"What did he say?" asked Faithful Night.

"He's rather eccentric, sir," I explained. "In fact he's bonkers."

"Let him speak!"

Pilgrim World must have caught him and pulled off the binding around his head because the next minute Saffron Tinker's voice flooded the void like a sluice gate opening: "...telling me her old lies and expecting me to believe them, 'What's the matter with you,' I said to her, 'do you think I'm crazy, you old crow, put the bedroom light on will you, you slut so as I can see your ugly mug to belt you one,' says I and what does she do but light a match and sets the bed on fire with me in it and there I am tied hand and foot and the flames blistering the ceiling and licking the soles of my feet and she throws open the window roaring with laughter into the night, 'Laugh will you?' says I as I fry like a trout in butter, but she says, 'Have you enough light now, you odious crab,' and I'm telling you now that..."

"Shut up, Saffron Tinker," I said, lashing out a smack in his direction.

"Ouch you bastard!" cried Pilgrim World whose nose got in the way.

"Now, now," said Faithful Night, "none of that here! And Saffron Tinker, you pull yourself together, if you want to see the light of day again."

"'Light,' he says," shouted Saffron Tinker. "'Light,' he says, the lying devil; you're the one who's stolen the light; bring it back to me or I'll trample you to smithereens, d'you hear, you cunning swine, where've you hidden it, I'll kill you, you bogeyman and who're all these other people, go to hell the bloody lot of you, go on, before I beat you all to a pulp."

"That's enough, unless you want the mouth rag," I said and surprisingly Saffron Tinker shut up.

"When the wise go astray they lose the way," commented Faithful Night with a sigh.

"He never was wise," said Pilgrim.

"What's this work you've got lined up for us?" I asked. "Does it pay?"

"Pay?" There was disbelief in Faithful Night's voice. "Is the honour of serving your people not enough reward for you, Gwern Excuses?"

"The hell it is. What have they ever done free for me?"

"Fine. We shall therefore have to hand you over to the Heartless Bodies who I understand are keen to meet you. I am sure you will be warmly welcomed by Befehlnotstand and his henchmen, perhaps even by Rausman personally, I shouldn't wonder."

"What do you want me to do, sir?" I said.

"Could you turn on the lights now please, if you see fit?" pleaded Pilgrim.

"There is no light down here therefore I do not see fit to do any such thing. My senses are tuned to people's hearts which I find quite sufficient to know them, light or no light."

"I don't believe you," I said. "What's in our friend Pilgrim's heart, if you're so clever?"

"In his heart there's a river flowing uphill," said Faithful Night.

"What do you mean?" asked Pilgrim. "What about Saffron Tinker, does he have a heart?"

"Oh, yes. In his heart there's a wild river flowing into a deep cave."

"Don't give me that crap," I laughed weakly. "What's in my heart then? Tell me that?"

"In your heart there is a river flowing between valley meadows with trees hanging over it, Gwern, and a ruined cottage on its banks with brambles breaking through the windows."

"I'm not going to listen to this twaddle," I said sharply. "Tell us what you want or let us go!"

"Calm down now, Gwern," said the voice slowly. "You've done quite well up to now, don't blow it." He took a moment then continued. "As you are no doubt aware by now, Rausman has ordered Befehlnotstand to mass the Heartless Bodies along the borders of the Exile States and the forecast is that there will soon be another strike against the Alliance."

"We heard something about that," I said.

"Well, now that you have won back Rock Jaw's allegiance to Small Country and the rest..."

"Forgive me," I butted in, "but all he did was agree to restore the supply he'd stolen and..."

"Exactly. You see, Rock Jaw has always been something of a black sheep but now he's back in the fold where he belongs, thanks to you! I'm sure Grind Underfoot's face was a sight worth seeing when you told him Rock Jaw sent him his regards."

"He got angry because he thought Gwern was having him on," said Pilgrim.

"I also note that you have to some extent pacified the Swarthy Cavedwarves. It was no mean feat to get them on your side. So now listen, I have advised the Answer Keeper to appoint you three as War Envoys to consult the members of the Alliance and to carry the message to mobilise forces! Are you willing and able?"

"I'll have a go," I said, "but I don't know if I can manage it with these two clowns for assistants."

"The boy wants to go alone, wants to go alone he does, alone it is he wants to go, let him go alone, yes, yes, he's to go all on his own, that's it, that's it, that's it..."

"Be quiet, Saffron Tinker," said the voice in an official tone. "You must all go together."

"Does that include me, sir?" asked Pilgrim World and I hissed "Hush now" in his ear for being silly.

"Put out your hand, Gwern," said the voice and I felt the cool roughness of the tunnel wall beneath my fingers. "The steps are to the left, some way down. Tell no one of your mission, send nothing through the wires. Oh, and you'd better leave your mobile processor here, Gwern, just in case. Grind Underfoot will provide all you need for your journey. I shall expect you back here in due course. Do you all understand? Gwern?"

"Understood, sir."

"Saffron Tinker?"

"Yes, it's him, I'm sure it is, what is the charge this time?"

"Pilgrim?"

"May I have the question again, sir, so I can be sure of the answer?"

By the time we reached the head of the stairs the sun was high in the sky, making us squint through our fingers. It was downhill all the way to New Village and we went straightaway to Leather Belly's place where we ordered as much as we could eat and drink and the best rooms in the house to sleep out the day and sleep out the night.

Testimony Four

That night we were woken by Dave Egg Stealer who said he had travelled far and wide in search of us.

"Thought you might like to hear these," he said, chucking four tapes onto my bed.

"Oh, great, some new releases!" said Pilgrim World from the other bed. "Anything by the Compromisers? We only get to hear old fashioned stuff up here."

"Oh shut up, Pilgrim," said Egg Stealer. "Come on, hurry up, we can listen to them in the sound chamber. Just leave Saffron Tinker wherever he is. Hey, Gwern, you're on these tapes, y'know and so is Fischermädchen. I had a hell of a job getting my hands on them."

"What if the Listeners get to know?"

"They don't suspect a thing, Gwern. Stroke of luck for once. Come on, let's go!"

He'd got a special pass that would admit him to anywhere in Lowland, he told us, given to him personally by Faithful Night, so he said. Penetrated the depths of the Listeners' underground chambers and lifted these four tapes and copied them before anyone could detect or suspect a thing. We were supposed to believe him, I guess, but Dave Egg Stealer never tells the whole truth, seems like he just can't face it anymore, which could be seen as a bonus in his position, being a spy. Suspect everyone and expect everyone to suspect you, that was his philosophy. But he must trust us at least. He's from Lowland after all, so they say.

Leather Belly was too busy in bed with a visitor from the border regions to serve us that late so we helped ourselves to a bottle of spirits and legged it over to the sound chamber. It was a good thing too that we took it as we would never have stayed awake in that warmth without it, not at five in the morning, slouched in the deep and cozy seats of the auditorium.

"Stick a tape in the player," said Dave Egg Stealer, throwing one of them at Pilgrim. I slumped back into the seat with my legs over the back of the one in front as the chamber began to echo like a cave with the clicking and whirring of the wires, broken suddenly by the familiar rasp of Fischermädchen's voice all around us.

"...Gwern, at last! Where have you been? I've been waiting for your call."

"I know. I'll be round first thing in the morning, don't worry. Does this have anything to do with the network contract? Look, I did say I wasn't too sure about that new software, didn't I? Are they really that annoyed?"

"Tomorrow morning, eight o'clock. Cool down, Gwern. Come at eight, everything is fine."

"I didn't know you'd been on radio, Gwern," said Pilgrim World but Dave Egg Stealer raised a finger to his lips.

The wires clicked and whirred and through them came her voice again, this time cold and purposeful:

"Bettnachzieher!"

"He is in bed, Madam Fischermädchen."

"Well get him up!"

"We're not sure whose bed he's sleeping in tonight, Madam Fischermädchen."

"Then put me through to General Befehlnotstand."

"Do you have a security clearance code, Madam Fischermädchen?"

"Twelve twenty two sixty six. Now put me through, you cheap little trollop before I get angry."

"Right away, Madam Fischermädchen."

Some strange music came through the wires and then we heard a man's gravelly voice,

"Fischermädchen. I presume that this is important."

"General Befehlnotstand, my apologies for troubling you. Bettnachzieher was 'unavailable'. I had no option but to come through to you, sir. General Befehlnotstand, the slippery eel has swallowed the bait. I shall be drawing in the line at eight tomorrow morning. You may send the Heartless Bodies!"

"Hmmmm. Well as it happens, Bettnachzieher is here with me, discussing strategy. Fortunately he is one of the few who are not tied to their desks. I will advise him of the situation. By eight tomorrow everything will be in place."

"Thank you Genera..." The line closed.

"Swine," cursed Fischermädchen.

"Haven't you got any tapes with pictures?" asked Pilgrim. "These are so boring."

"What d'you want, the penny and the bun?" asked Dave Egg Stealer. "Get lost if you're going to moan. Stick the next tape in, instead of yawning like a catfish."

"What's a catfish?"

"Just do it!"

Again the speakers crackled and spat static and then came the sound of heavy breathing.

"General Befehlnotstand, General Befehlnotstand! Thank God you picked up the phone!"

"Good morning, Fischermädchen. Ask one of the Heartless Bodies to bring the little worm to the phone and have him hurt badly so I can hear him squirm. I have been looking forward to this."

"General Befehlnotstand, he didn't show up. The Heartless

Bodies have been to his lodgings. We've had the place turned over. The bird has flown."

"Fischermädchen, I am disappointed in you. I shudder to think what Rausman will have to say about this. I would not wish to be in your shoes right now. I want the contents of his network screen personal information file downloaded to me here immediately! I shall have his details on every screen from Entwürdigung City to Bhaarata. The little fox will not get far."

"General Befehlnotstand, the little fox has wiped the hard disk. All that remains is a foul message suggesting that I perform a lewd act with 'my fish', sir."

"You are losing your grip, Fischermädchen. It seems you have blown your cover this time. The Lowlanders are starting to lose faith in you. Perhaps it is something in your voice? What is it about you? You were fully trained and briefed. A waste of time! I hold you personally responsible for this. You have three days to find the insect's habitat and to crush it under your heel, otherwise you'll find yourself in a totally different kettle of fish! Do I make myself clear, Fischermädchen?"

"Perfectly, General Befehlnotstand. Firstly, may I exp..."

The customary click closed the line, leaving only the phone's tone as a background to Fischermädchen's slow, deliberate swearing in language so exalted and pure that I could scarcely make out a single word.

"You really dropped her in it, didn't you," commented Dave Egg Stealer. "I'm not saying she didn't deserve it, the toffee-nosed shrew. Sharp of you to format that hard disk, Gwern, all credit where it's due."

"I had the code," I replied. "Any door can be opened with the right key. By the way, how are things down in Lowland by now? Is there much talk of war down there?"

"Are you mad? Talk of war has been banned under Lowland Council resolution seven two seven. They don't want to aggravate the Exile States now, do they? And that toilet paper with Befehlnotstand's face on it has been withdrawn. It looks as though it won't be long before things start to hot up down there. Why else would Befehlnotstand's forces be gathering along the borders and his Heartless Bodies on 'manoeuvres' in the area? I heard Rausman himself recently addressed an assembly of his slaves to celebrate the Exile States' forever-freedom anniversary. Oh yes, I can see it coming, boy."

"But Lowland is supposed to be free now," said Pilgrim. "They don't have to fight."

"Oh, I see, Pilgrim, of course," replied Dave Egg Stealer. "Lowland is free. I forgot. Free to follow in the footsteps of the Exile States and imitate them every step of the way. Free to acquiesce and to bow down low, is that what you mean? Free to agree but not to differ. You've hit the nail on the head again, Pilgrim, of course they don't have to fight. They can put their hands up like last time as Befehlnotstand lines them up against a wall. He only wants their land anyway, he's not interested in the people, I read that in the papers."

"It won't come to war," said Pilgrim World sulkily.

"You'd be shot for saying that in the Exile States," snapped Egg Stealer. "But then you'd probably have been shot ages ago for an idiot. Play the third tape and stop pissing about."

Click, went the tape and out came Fischermädchen's voice talking our language, her accent creaking like a swollen door.

"Well, hello, Scarlet Nightshade, long time, no see?"

"Fischermädchen? I was about to phone you…"

"Well you didn't, did you? You are a fickle girl. Would you betray me?"

"My God, no, Fischermädchen, never! Didn't you see my report? What's wrong?"

"It's you that's wrong, Scarlet Nightshade, only you. I'm not sure I can still depend on you any more."

"Of course you can, definitely; I wouldn't double cross you, Fischermädchen, you know that..."

"Prove it. I want to know about Gwern Excuses. You do know him, don't you."

"In passing. Enough to say 'hello'."

"Enough to say, 'Just go. Go back to your Little Caress Heart and see if she'll take you in'?"

"How did you know about that?"

"Being thick is not a qualification for my job, Scarlet Nightshade, but knowing the long and the short of your lies, that is an essential qualification, wouldn't you agree?"

"What do you want of me?"

"I want to know about Gwern Excuses."

"You know more than I do."

"Perhaps."

"What use am I to you then?"

"You are my eyes and my ears, Scarlet Nightshade. Now open that beak and start singing."

"I don't know him that well. If I'd known him better he never would have stolen my heart. He took it before I knew it. Then he threw it down and crushed it."

"He did that, did he, Scarlet?"

"He loves Caress more than me. He always loved her, the little bitch, long before he ever pretended to care for me. He never loved me properly, not even in bed. Refused my arms, saying 'I don't want to hurt you,' over and again: every word like a knife turning within me. I didn't know him at all."

"Do you know him now?"

"Perhaps... how should I know?"

"Why do you defy me, my pretty? I am your friend. Who else has stood up for you? You can trust me, Scarlet."

"I know. I'm sorry, Fischermädchen. It was Wil Pickled Herring who broke my necklace and beat me up, not Gwern. He wouldn't have done that. Wil Pickled Herring got jealous seeing me talking to Gwern on Town Square. He's a wild one, when he's pissed, same as when he's sober."

"I'm not interested in some pickled prat. Don't change the subject. What did Gwern Excuses say to you on Town Square that got Wil Pickled Herring going?"

"Gwern told me he'd done something bad in the Exile States and that he'd wrecked some software or somesuch, all that stuff is really beyond me. Said it was all a mistake but that the Heartless Bodies would soon be on to him so he wasn't going to hang around. Didn't seem too bothered, mind. 'They still don't know it was me corrupted the system,' he said, cocky like. 'And anyway, I'm not afraid of the Heartless Bodies.' 'Why you shivering then?' says I. 'Because you're standing so close, Scarlet,' he smarms up to me. 'Get away from there, Scarlet!' said Wil Pickled Herring, crossing over from the White Wheat Tavern towards us. 'Get away from the little traitor.' He grabbed me by the arm to pull me away. 'Who are you calling a traitor you drunken scum?' said Gwern looking him straight in the eye. I shrugged off Wil's grasp but he snatched at my necklace and pulled me down into the subway where the necklace burst, then he grabbed me by the hair and dragged me out the other side where he hit me in the face but I got free and ran off. I ran and ran to my sister's house and I didn't go back to pick up the beads till I was sure Wil Pickled Herring would be pickled senseless outside All Night Café and out for the count. That's the last time I saw Gwern."

"In the subway?"

"Yes."

"Good girl. You see, I know already. Nice to see you're telling the truth for once. Where did he go afterwards?"

"I've told you, I don't know. Home I guess. Or to see Caress. Ask her. Don't ask me."

"He's pretty close to her, isn't he?"

"You're telling me! Far too close for his own good. I would have been better for him. And everybody knows she's head over heels *with him but that the little fool won't forgive him. What's a bit of playing the field? It's in his blood, but she just doesn't get it. She wants it all or nothing, that's Little Caress Heart. Who the hell does she think she is, Miss High and Mighty strutting around Town Square when everyone knows he's the father?"*

"Gwern is Calonnog's father?"

"Who else? You knew that already, anyway. Everybody knows that."

"Yes, I knew. Of course. Our little chat has been illuminating. Is that the time? Goodbye now, Scarlet. Remember now to phone me before I have to phone you."

Fischermädchen must have put the phone down really carefully because there was only the lightest click as the line closed.

"Bit of a fly by night," said Dave Egg Stealer smugly. "What's done by night is seen by day. Did you know about all this, Pilgrim?"

"It's none of my business," said Pilgrim.

"That's right," I said, "so just shut up, Egg Stealer. I wouldn't throw stones if I lived where you do. We'll all get to know soon enough what you've been up to once the nursery schools start filling up with your offspring."

"That was below the belt," pouted Dave Egg Stealer.

"He that sows brambles should not walk barefoot," commented Pilgrim World philosophically.

"Out of the mouths of babes…" I added. "Put the last tape in, Pilgrim, and leave the scholarly stuff to the scholars."

There was a terrible scratching sound when the last tape began but this was cleared with the bleep of an answer machine. Then came the shock of my own voice from another age chirping like a cricket:

"Gwern here. Sorry I can't take your call. Leave a message after the tone…."

"Pilgrim World hereby summons Gwern Excuses to an audience with Bonebleach right away in Sunless Summer."

"That was me!" shouted Pilgrim, hitting the stop button. "Remember that, Gwern? Can we hear it again?"

"No I don't and no you can't," I said.

"But you told Bonebleach that you'd got the message."

"How come you remember all the trivia and none of the big picture, Pilgrim? Ok, so I lied. Who cares? If I had listened to the message you can bet I'd never have come. Now hit the button and shut up."

Next came Fischermädchen's voice spitting venom into my little machine:

"Gwern Excuses. Where are you? Wake up! It's gone eight o'clock! Why didn't you come on time? You must come right now, immediately!"

"These tapes are in the wrong order," I said.

"Don't complain," said Dave Egg Stealer. "You know the order. Here's the last part."

"Who's on this one then?"

"If you shut up you'll hear..."

"...not here." (It was your voice, Caress: how could I have interrupted your opening words?)

"Has he been there?" demanded Fischermädchen.

"What's the big deal?"

"Listen, Caress, we're worried about him. He should have been here at eight this morning. He did not come. We are concerned that something may have happened to him."

"Yeah, yeah, I bet! Why would you worry about him? What's he to you?"

"What is he to you, Caress? You tell me that and I will tell you the truth too."

"You lot from the Exile States know everything, don't you?"

"Yes, Caress, I may be from the Exile States, but I've your interests at heart. You know that. This is a bad time in Lowland's history. Your new freedom is fragile and I am here on your behalf to ensure its future. Gwern has been quite naughty to trash the tidy network our friends across the border kept up so well. But I know he didn't do it on purpose and that's why I want to help him before he really pisses off Befehlnotstand and the Heartless Bodies, if you'll excuse the colloquialism."

"I'm saying nothing. I know nothing. Befehlnotstand will never get his claws into him and neither will the Heartless Bodies."

"Don't you be too sure, Caress. I'd certainly hate to think what they'd do to him should he fall into their clutches before he got the chance to say sorry. A circle of steel surrounds Lowland; he cannot get away, the net is closing in on him. Don't you want to help him?"

"He meant no harm, Fischermädchen, you said that yourself. We all know how headstrong he can be, but he's not really against the Exile States, no matter what he blabbers in his drink."

"You will help him, won't you?"

"I don't want him to get hurt."

"You love him very much, don't you Caress?"

"I do, but the boy is fickle like spring rain, and the showers don't always fall on me."

"He's been unfaithful."

"He thinks I don't know what he's up to. But I hear all about him from Scarlet Nightshade. At least she's a true friend."

"Does he know that you still love him?"

"I don't want him to know. Don't want him using my heart in his book of broken hearted ballards. I've told him not to come here any more. But I do want to help him, Fischermädchen, I don't want him to get hurt. I reckon he's making tracks for Small

Country, he's often said that's where he'd go if things got too hot for him around here. Do you think he'll make it?"

"Not a hope in hell. But if I manage to reach him before Befehlnotstand and his Heartless Bodies at least I can get him to give himself up to Rausman's Counsellors and that will stand in his favour at his trial."

"Thank you for helping us, Fischermädchen. I'm sorry I was a bit suspicious of you earlier on."

"Caress.. this is confidential, but there is talk that this will lead to war. No one will be safe then. Especially those who've been close to Gwern Excuses. I suggest that you and the boy, Calonnog isn't it, should come under my wing here where you know you will both be safe. What d'you say?"

"War? All out war? Not over something so trivial? It was an accident, even you said that. What do they want from us?"

"You will come then?"

"I'll stay here until I know that Gwern is safe."

"That's a shame. I thought you had more sense."

"Scarlet Nightshade is staying put. She says she won't move. Calonnog and I will be fine here at Helen's Stone, thank you."

"You are a stubborn girl. But remember what I said, Caress, I'll take you in any time. If you insist on holing up in that dank valley, that's up to you. I'm sure Scarlet Nightshade will look after you."

The line clicked and closed for the last time leaving me staring into space with your voice still ringing in my ears. I was silently cursing Scarlet Nightshade for her lies and Fischermädchen for her deception. Slowly I came to, hurting all over to think that you still loved me and knowing that I loved you but that life had made us like two magnets, pushing each other aside.

"That's the lot," Dave Egg Stealer cut through my dreams' cobwebs. He yawned lazily and added, "The bottle's empty and the night is gone. You've heard it all now, Gwern. What're you going to do?"

"Rescue her from that poisonous Scarlet Nightshade and

Fischermädchen, that's what, Egg Stealer, and I don't care how long it takes."

"First we've got to visit the Alliance countries," interjected Pilgrim as he took the last tape out.

"I know, I know, as if I could forget!"

"You what?" said Dave Egg Stealer.

"It's a secret," I explained. "We have to persuade the alliance countries to join forces with Small Country before all hell breaks loose."

"I get it, but why on earth would they send you? Is that stinky Saffron Tinker going too? The three rusty queers, for Christ's sake. Here's hoping you have fun!"

"No need to get nasty, just 'cause you're not invited," I said. "Just because we get to visit all sorts of exotic places, every country under the sun. Hey, Pilgrim, you packed the suntan lotion? Good lad." I did my best to make Egg Stealer jealous, gilding it with all the details of our trip to the Earth Vineyard where we'd get to meet Duke Waronket Kalz, and then onwards to the Great Vineyard to General Bol's court (not forgetting to bring exquisite delicacies as presents for him), after which we'd go to Long Island where we'd insist upon an audience with the renowned prince Gonéirín Bóthar-Leat and onwards again after that, this time by air to Bhaarata to arrange an audience with the Emperor Baraa Haathi. I explained that this was where the suntan lotion would come in handy, probably also sunglasses and a punka-wallah. This is how I boasted about our journey, no way did I reckon it would actually happen. Not with two nutters for assistants. Come to think of it, Saffron Tinker was still stinking in his bed where we'd left him in Leather Belly's attic where the rainwater dripped down on him from the rafters and soaked his beard while he slept.

So big deal, he had to split, said Dave Egg Stealer, he was not officially here in the first place. Sworn to secrecy I sent Pilgrim World to fetch Saffron Tinker before anyone else woke up. We made our farewells in the early light of day, Dave Egg Stealer dressed up as a Moral Standards Inspector, setting off in one direction and Saffron Tinker, Pilgrim and myself riding out the other side of town. It was only much later, when we got back and Faithful Night had given me back my mobile processor, that I set down the details. It wasn't that he doubted we'd make it through, it's just that it was quite an expensive piece of equipment and he didn't want it to get lost, that's what he told me. Anyway, here I am sitting at my little desk under the window tapping all these details into my machine.

Testimony Five

We only arrived back the night before last. A new moon hung among the stars as we rode our mules out of New Village towards the mountain and the door in the rock. Our mission would not be over until we delivered our report to Faithful Night in the Lower Level. Though we had wandered distant lands and roamed the far countries, even seasoned travellers like us couldn't negotiate the rough paths to Faithful Night's door without a full moon. I sent Pilgrim World back to New Village to get us an electric torch each from Grind Underfoot's storehouse, and that was how we found the entrance and the deep stairway.

We tied the mules to some spindly bushes on the summit before descending the stone steps to the Lower Level, torch in hand. The deeper we went down, the weaker the light of the torches became until all we had left were three green specks like glow worms which were soon enough swallowed by the velvet blackness.

"Welcome back," said Faithful Night's voice in my ear when once again we stood in the void he called home. "What news, my long lost friends?"

"Trials and tribulations, troubles," blurted out Saffron Tinker, raising his voice as he spoke. "Misfortune, pain, sorrow oh God, sir, these two were indeed useless. Oh yes, and she was in my head all the time too, contradicting me and cursing me, I'm telling you, if a man could only be allowed peace to draw breath, hell it's come to something when..."

"That's enough, Saffron Tinker," commanded the voice. "When I require your opinion I shall ask for it. In the meantime, Gwern, accord me your report, concisely and to the point."

"May I ask something at this juncture?" asked Pilgrim hopefully.

"No you can't," I told him but he asked anyway.

"What do you mean by 'accord', exactly?"

"Shut up!" said Faithful Night. "Or I'll freeze the very tongue in your head. And yours too, Saffron Tinker, if either of you interrupt your leader again! Gwern...?"

"At once, Faithful Night, sir," I replied, scratching my chin, sorry that Faithful Night hadn't allowed me the use of my mobile processor to record the journey. "Well, sir, we have in general terms accomplished most of what you told us to do, I think, sir. We slithered like vipers through the lands of the Alliance in the guise of war envoys under your patronage: no one crossed us. Our first destination was Earth Vineyard, south across the sea. That's where we met Duke Waronket Kalz and his two henchmen, Mewdall Bemdez and Revrad Bemnoz. Don't they have fine houses in Earth Vineyard? We'd been nosing around, not wanting to draw attention to ourselves when we met the itinerant Stoty Vragoù who put us on the right trail.

'Come zis vey,' he said and so we followed him. Stoty Vragoù can worm his way even into the kingdom's closest hiding places, apparently. He said, 'Be as wagabonds viz me. You will be made welcome by Waronket Kalz.' We found that Waronket Kalz did not know too much but what he knew he knew well.

'Come sit at ze table,' Waronket Kalz told the four of us. 'A glass each for ze bread seekers. Give them each a two pound loaf and meat and potatoes, as much as they can take! Did you know, vanderers, there are tales told about your kind coming like this across the sea to the palace of the Duke. They were called Al Lostig from Ploureos and Paket Omp from Gwitalneblec'h; both had lost their way. You should hear the story. We've not heard of anyone like them until this day and so velcome and one hundred velcomes to Earth Wineyard. Come, Unan All'ta, bring cups, let the cider flow, uncork the wine that our guests may drink in liberal and generous measure!'

'We appreciate the welcome,' I answered in an appropriately

formal syntax. 'I won't deny that we're thirsty.'

To cut a long story short, that's how we spent the rest of the evening, carousing and feasting and making merry. Then the duke's daughter came forward, a lovely smiling maiden.

'I'm Over Easy,' she said with a curtsy to Pilgrim.

'Well I'm not; sorry, not that way inclined,' said the bone-head, crying off with a headache from all that wine and cider. Then Saffron Tinker started up, railing against the loose morals of contemporary society, so I went to keep Lady Over Easy company in her rooms high in the tower. There we spent a most agreeable night, sipping wine and making polite conversation and doing the things tradition demands of such situations.

The next day, mid morning in the kitchen, who'd I find but Saffron Tinker snoring away on the table and Pilgrim World in a huge sulk because I'd stolen his girlfriend! What is he like? Where do you think I found Duke Waronket Kalz? With his henchmen, Revrad Bemnoz and Mewdall Bemdez comparing vintages and trumpeting the exploits of their tribe before Rausman and Befehlnotstand and the Heartless Bodies put paid to their antics.

'Duke Waronket Kalz, friend, mentor,' I said in my grave official voice. 'I find it intriguing that you should mention the Exile States, for that is why we are here... no, do not be afraid, we are not Heartless Bodies but war envoys sent from the Small Country to convey to you as our allies the news of a great wave of rearmament and mobilisation on our borders. Here under official seal direct from the high authority of Faithful Night, is what you have to do. Unite with us to turn back this tide and on the hearths of Earth Vineyard and in her halls the legends of your exploits will echo down the ages, not the exploits of two half baked bums like Al Lostig and Packed Omp!'

'What on earth do you mean?' stuttered Waronket Kalz, sobering up straight. 'What can we do against so many when we are so small? Who will stand by us in our hour of need? No, I'm afraid that...'

'Duke Waronket Kalz, we have with us already Small Country,

the Swarthy Cavedwarves and the Wire Bandits, not to mention Lowland, Great Vineyard, Long Island and Bhaarata.'

'Ha! So you come to us last of all! Well no one shall call Earth Vineyard a country of cowards! Is not our blood as red as the rest? We will be there!'

'I never doubted that you would, sir.'

Having bade farewell to Duke Waronket Kalz and his court we went to try our luck in the Great Vineyard. It was Saffron Tinker who messed things up for us there, and only by the skin of our teeth did we keep the contract. As you know, Faithful Night, sir, he is a native of that country, but since wandering the backroads of this world so long, he could hardly remember a word of his mother tongue at first."

"This boy is a liar and a devil in a man's skin making mischief again and again and..." shouted Tinker, getting agitated in the darkness.

"One more word, Saffron Tinker," snapped Faithful Night and we heard Saffron Tinker's jaws snap to like a mousetrap.

"Well, anyway," I went on, "the roads in Great Vineyard are very long and we had our share of walking. It took us ages to reach the President's HQ on Vineyard Island. Well, we were hardly any wiser then because that place is like an ants' nest, no exaggeration. Everyone darting from one place to another and nobody willing to pause for breath to give us directions, they didn't even seem to notice us, sir. And didn't Saffron Tinker have to start up his nonsense calling them names and shouting obscenities, and at the top of his voice and what's worse, in their own language. It was touch and go they didn't cut off our heads because of him, but that's another story. Suffice to say that eventually we were dragged before Général Bol in the high chambers where he holds court.

'Well tell him what we are doing here, Saffron Tinker,' I demanded of this one and d'you know what he replied?

'Good day to you all and I'm fed up of this too,' he said. 'A war about to break and everyone diving for cover while you lot wolf down foie gras and vintage claret and all you can think about is your stupid grammatical rules, shame on you, you materialistic turkeys, I'd rather wander alone an eccentric tinker with nothing between my ears save what got there to begin with; now, are you with us or not, you cheese eaters?'

'What's this?' cried Général Bol, tearing the napkin from his collar and pushing aside his table. 'What's this tripe, lard heads!'

I explained as best I could in my broken Great Vineyardish and as I did so I noticed Général Bol's nostrils flaring wider at each mispronounced syllable.

'Est bien,' he said finally, once I'd told him of our welcome in the Earth Vineyard, and he called Où Suis-Je his servant to show us to our lodgings.

Superb accommodation, it was too. Drapes of silk and silk wallpaper, all with a pis-en-lit pattern. I was worried how this might affect Pilgrim, but I needn't have, he didn't even notice. We had a bedroom each off the best parlour and a four poster bed in each room with a bottle of fine spirits the colour of sunlight through autumn leaves by the side of each bed.

'What shall we do next?' asked Pilgrim but before I could answer there came a knock on the door and in came three of the prettiest girls.

'Good evening, gentlemen,' said the tall black-haired blue-eyed one, holding her handkerchief to her nose. Who could blame her; Saffron Tinker never seems to wash.

'You've got the wrong room, girls,' said Pilgrim in his wide-eyed way. I didn't bother translating.

'On the game, are you, you brazen hussies?' shouted Saffron Tinker. He didn't open his mouth again that night.

'Go to bed, Pilgrim,' I said. 'We'll fetch a doctor for Saffron Tinker in a minute, girls.'

'I can't stand the sight of blood,' said the tall black-haired blue-eyed one. 'Let us introduce ourselves,' she added. 'I am Ilyena de Monde, this is Silte Plais and here is Ellée Belle. How best may we entertain you?'

'Forget the formal-speak, honey,' I said and suggested to Pilgrim he might as well go to his room. Saffron Tinker was still lying on his back in a coma with his tongue sticking out. Perhaps I did hit him a bit too hard, but he's used to it by now. Anyway, you're a busy man, Faithful Night, sir, so I won't bore you with all the details. Suffice to say we passed an entertaining night and in the moring the three of them got dressed and off they went. I called down for a room service breakfast.

Breakfast is an understatement, though. All you get is a dry croissant and a tiny cup of black coffee, hardly enough to drown a flea. Général Bol was in high spirits when we got downstairs.

'Good day to you,' he said brightly. 'Overnight I had the opportunity to mull things, over, fortified by a dish of quails in truffle sauce. I have spoken over the wires with Waronket Kalz and rather than get left out again I am prepared to support and unite with the Alliance on condition that the Grand Vignoblais shall be the official language of this historic repulse of... ehm, sorry, who was it we might be fighting?'

'My liege, you probably should not have discussed such matters over the telephone,' I pointed out. 'No doubt the cat is now some distance from the bag.'

'Do not worry, my boy, Waronket Kalz and I have an understanding. The Listeners on the other hand understand neither of us.' That is what he said, Faithful Night, sir..."

"He's a silly coot by God," shouted Saffron Tinker wildly. "He's all riddles and rhymes. All he does from dawn to dusk is stoke up his fat belly and..."

"This is your last warning, Saffron Tinker," said Faithful Night, his voice sharp as ice.

"Well, sir," I went on, "this is how it was after that. We were given a lift to the city gates by Vadonc Andouille, the transport minister and on we went from there in the direction of Long Island.

Once we reached the coast we took the ferry. On board we changed into the grand silk suits we'd found in Général Bol's wardrobe. I must admit we did look pretty fine, we were even invited by the Captain to dine with him at the top table with all the marine bigwigs. Pilgrim World embarrassed us by being sick under the table and spoiling the captain's calf-skin shoes. I'd locked up Saffron Tinker in our cabin and when I got poor Pilgrim back to put him to bed it turned out Saffron Tinker'd gone completely off his head and had tried to light a fire to dry out the water he could see outside his port hole, thinking he'd wet the bed. Thank God we docked next morning by the quayside at Long Island, where I asked a little chap if he knew how we might find the Prince.

'Sure, but that's me,' he exclaimed, all exited. 'Come and wet your whistle, am I not croaking for a pint myself? Are you thirsty?'

'Yes,' said Saffron Tinker, his eyes rolling strangely.

'No,' said I.

'Yes and no,' faltered Pilgrim.

The little chap on the quay turned out to be Céas Thú Féin and not the Prince at all; he'd only wanted to tell us what we wanted to hear, seeing how we'd come such a long way. 'I'll take you to him, though, right enough,' he added with a wink and we followed him, more fool us.

We followed him to Bás le Tart's house, which turned out to be an inn packed with serious drinkers knocking back pint after pint of dark even though it was only six in the morning with the dawn mist still nibbling the street corners.

'Let's have some Sean Nós singing, Bído Thost!' shouted Céas Thú Féin at an old grey man in the corner. 'Only the best for our finely dressed noble visitors who honour this splendid morning. Say your song and say it well!' Every head in the room turned to glance at us but their pints were more interesting. Bído Thost sang his song, an interminable ballad whose pure notes were drowned by the clamouring of the Long Islanders' setting the world to rights.

'And where d'you three come from then?' asked a man wearing a cloth cap whose nose was a tuck-knife in the middle of his face. 'Sure, I can see you're no Heartless Bodies, anyways.'

'Indeed we are not,' confirmed Pilgrim. 'We can sing!'

'From Small Country,' I explained carefully, trying not to spill the beans. But I'm afraid my tongue had been rather loosened by too much water of life. 'We're here to speak with the Prince!' I boasted.

'Gonéirín Bóthar-Leat?' asked the man. 'Sure as my name's Cé Tá Rá'gat, the very same will be here now at seven this morning. He comes here on the dot each day on his way to the House of Assembly. Now throw that west, my friends, and have another one.'

By the time Prince Gonéirín Bóthar-Leat arrived at seven, Saffron Tinker was up to his tricks again, and Pilgrim World had started to make up all sorts of stories, showing off to the brothers Tar and Amach Anseo, telling them he was originally from Long Island and could drink anyone under the table. I'm sorry I was too drunk to stem his flow.

All Gonéirín Bóthar-Leat had to do was put one foot over the threshold and the whole house hushed like the grave. Bás le Tart took up a pin he probably kept for the purpose and let it drop to the floor with a tiny tinkle. The threshold ceremony over, everyone started up their shouting again as Gonéirín Bóthar-Leat muscled his way in through the packed bodies to the bar.

'Gentlemen to see you, Prince,' said Bás le Tart, drawing a slow pint of white and black and marking a cross on the slate above the till.

'Have they made an appointment?'

'Doubt it.'

'Sure, that's fine then, where are they?'

'By your elbow, dear Prince, here they are. Gwern Excuses, Mad Saffron Tinker and Pilgrim, come all the way from Small Country to our fair island just to see you, so they say.'

'God bless you and a hundred thousand welcomes,' said Prince Gonéirín Bóthar-Leat, quaffing a draught of his pint. 'What tidings?'

I explained as best I could, what with Pilgrim World butting in every minute boasting of his Long Island ancestry. He's a wise man, that Gonéirín Bóthar-Leat. Mid morning saw me only half way through my report so he sent Goraibh Maith'gat the Agriculture Minister to postpone the morning debate in the House of Assembly. By mid afternoon he'd also sent Nabí Magadh from Sliabh Garbh to declare an international amnesty for under age drinkers.

'Let me introdush Saffron Tinker to shomeone special,' he declared at around four o'clock as the afternoon began to fade when a towering redheaded woman in a green dress shoved everyone out of her way, planting herself on a stool and her elbow on the bar. 'Shaffron Tinker... I want to introdush my shishter, Támé Íngráleat... Támé Íngráleat, this is my friend Shaffron Tinker from Small Country, war envoy to Faithful Night, no less....'

You've got to believe us, Faithful Night, sir, we really would have been back ages ago if it hadn't been for that. Well, there's no point crying over spilt milk, and Saffron Tinker is much better now he has a fine wife in Támé Íngráleat, she really is a consolation to him in his dotage. But believe me, sir, I had no idea that the marriage feast would last a fortnight....

The long and the short of it is that the happy couple have rented a little summer cottage called Stone Hollow for the winter, their honeymoon, so to speak. That is, of course, once he has completed his service to you, sir, and if he gets his marbles back in order. I must admit though, that's a bit of an if to kick off with.

Well now, of course Gonéirín Bóthar-Leat agreed at once that he'd be on our side, sir. We got on famously with him. He took us to stay with him and Pilgrim used to wash the dishes while Saffron Tinker carried on with Támé Íngráleat and as for Gonéirín Bóthar-Leat and I, we pored over various strategies with a bottle of fifteen year old whisky for company. But listen, sir, that's how you've got to do business in Long Island, sir, and anyone who tells you two weeks is a long time to close a bargain with Gonéirín Bóthar-Leat, well, sir, he dosn't know Gonéirín Bóthar-Leat that well."

"May I say something now, please?" asked Pilgrim, pouncing on the pause.

"Is it relevant?" said the voice through the black air.

"Well, not exactly, but..."

"Be quiet then and shut up. So that was Long Island. Now the last of the alliance countries, Bhaarata, what progress there, Gwern?"

"Yes, well, after we parted from Gonéirín Bóthar-Leat, with the official seal of his House of Assembly tucked safely under my arm, we winged it to the airport and sorted a place on the Over Ocean. It was Gonéirín Bóthar-Leat's contacts that got us a seat in spite of the cutbacks and the wait-lists. He'd got us papers as undercover agents that gave us almost missionary status. It seemed to work as no one stood in our way, not even the airport taxi drivers.

'I've heard this is a very cold country,' said Saffron Tinker, wrapping his fur more tightly about him as we walked from the plane to the tunnel.

'At least you have the courage of your convictions,' I replied, rolling up my cotton shirt sleeves and taking a pair of sunglasses out of its case.

'I'd never even heard of the place,' said Pilgrim in his safari shorts and his sandals and a huge bear skin fur hat. 'I've always wanted to visit but it was too far to walk.'

As we dragged our luggage from the conveyor belt, goose-flesh standing out on my arms – and Pilgrim's legs – it looked like Saffron Tinker, smug in his warm fur coat, had been right all along. But once the glass doors slid open onto the street we walked into a Dowlais furnace and there was Saffron Tinker stripping off like the Moulin Rouge.

I asked the taxi-wallah if he'd take us to see Emperor Baraa Haathi but he just smiled and rolled his head like a wooden doll.

'My name is Meraa Deesa,' he said. 'I'm sure you'll want to see the Sundara Larakii's memorial in Sundara Nagara, friends, for that's where the tourist always go and that's where I'm taking you. It was built by Sundara Larakii's husband Shaah Kitanee Paisaa, to draw visitors to this place some time ago.'

'We are not going there,' I said.

'Yes, sabji,' said Meraa Deesa, 'all the tourists want to see the memorial built by Sundara Larakii's husband Shaah Kitanee Paisaa to draw the tourists to this place.'

'Stop the car!' I shouted. 'We are not tourists!'

'You want the bhang-wallah, sabji? Come, we'll go see the paan-wallah on Pansh Muurti corner under the shade of the pomegranate tree. He's got the best!'

'We're here to see Emperor Baraa Haathi,' I said, 'and if you don't take us to him you won't get paid!'

'Ac'chaa, sabji, sir, why didn't you say so in the first place?' At last the penny dropped and he took us straight.

The doorman, Chowkidar Pataa Nahii in his splendid red and gold turban led us into a hallway dark after the glare of the sun, up a flight of twisting stairs so narrow you had to squeeze up sideways on. At the top we reached a long dusty corridor with numbered doors opening off it.

'Office two four seven, enquiries,' said Pataa Nahii, raising a quivering palm to his forehead in salute.

'Thanks,' we said but he didn't move, just kept standing to attention, his head begining to roll ever so slightly.

We gave him three units for his trouble and went on into the office where a crowd of people waited their turn, some sitting, some jostling at the counter and others cross-legged in the middle of the room sharing lunch.

In the end we managed to register our presence; the official scribe called Meeraa Naama Oont-Hai opened a brand new file just for us, all dated and stamped.

'Fill in this form for me too, in triplicate, and bring back the pink copy,' he advised when he was ready. We took it back a few hours later.

We had to fight our way through a throng to his desk, waving the pink form above our heads to keep it tidy.

'Where's the General Certificate of Preferences?' he asked. We did not have one.

I sent Pilgrim across the city in a cycle rickshaw to pick up the certificate and by the time he got back the others were already unrolling their blankets and preparing for bed.

'Come back some other time,' said Meeraa Naama Oont-Hai.

'What d'you mean?' I asked with a sinking feeling. 'How long do we have to wait, venerable sir?'

'Tomorrow, day after, day after that,' he dismissed us with a lazy gesture.

'We are here on official business from Small Country,' I said angrily. 'You'll have to answer to Emperor Baraa Haathi for keeping us waiting like this.'

'What to do?' he replied gently. 'The brothers Garama and Thadaa Pani from Rajpur, they used to come day and night for forty years: did that get them anywhere? The reason they came was to petition Emperor Double Roti about water extraction rights in Meeraa Gaava and by the time they got to see him he'd long since been cremated and his son Baraa Haathi who knew nothing of the case had acceded to his place and could not find the files and sent them home empty handed.'

'Well, we haven't forty years to spare,' I said looking him in the eye. 'Just tell me whose palms need greasing.'

'In that case, tell me when you want to see him, sabji.'

'Tomorrow morning.'

'Ac'chaa, sabji.' He rubbed his chin thoughtfully. 'Give me one hundred units deposit and then go with Chowkidar Pataa Nahii to Parhanaa Likhanaa letterwriter on Badmarsh Larakii Square and give him this note together with two hundred more units and everything will be done by nine o'clock tomorrow morning. Ac'chaa?'

'We can't afford that,' I lied. 'You can have fifty units now and I'll give Parhanaa Likhanaa the letterwriter another hundred and we'll settle for ten o'clock. Ok?'

He looked mortified. 'Sabji, inflation is rife in Great Bhaarata. Pay ten per cent more, sabji and come by half past ten and it will all be arranged.'

'Bahuta ac'chaa,' I agreed and we shook hands.

The Emperor Baraa Haathi is a massive big man with a great black beard filling his face and a tall golden turban on his head and a long thin sword in a golden scabbard. He even has jewels fixed to his desk next to the phone. My guess is that he must have his own super-wide staircase or maybe he just doesn't go out. He dusted off our file and said, 'Chai wallah, tea for our guests.'

'Baraa Haathiji, Emperor of Sun and Earth and Great Bhaarata,' I announced after we'd had a glass each of sweet milky tea. 'A message from the Answer Keeper! The Heartless Bodies are massing on our borders and he wants to know will you join with us to push the Exile States back?'

'Oh, it was great here when the Exile States used to run our affairs,' exclaimed Baraa Haathi, a teardrop coming to his fierce eye. 'So wonderful, the discipline of the Heartless Bodies. Everything's all to pieces nowadays and no respect for anything or anybody. Are the trains running on time? They are not. Do the days and nights keep to their schedules? They do not. Is there one man left in this land who can make a proper white sauce anymore? There is not! Let them come this very day! The Heartless Bodies, Rausman and his Counsellors, they can all come and welcome, as long as they bring a cook with them. It would be so much less hassle for them to run this show for me again.'

'Oh brave Baraa Haathi-ji, Universal Emperor, Overlord of All, mightn't that mean you go down in history as a bit of a chicken?'

'You think so? Hmmmm... listen, I will do one thing. If there might be danger of losing face... I will send what I can spare from my army plus six circus elephants; that should make Answer Keeper happy. They are not trained to fight, though, remember. Only for show, tell him.'

'Thanks, Bara Hathi-ji,' said the three of us and called it a day."

"You seem to have carried out your duties fairly well," came Faithful Night's voice, "and although you have not told me everything about the journey, your story will do for now. Reach out with your right hand, Gwern, can you feel your mobile processor. It is updated for war. Go now and develop your skills in software engineering and other arts under Mandrake Moon, Commander of the Air Peaceforce; you, Pilgrim, had better go with him as an apprentice. Be in the Air Caves by seven. You, Saffron Tinker, are to complete your period of service minding the army's mules up on Bleak Heath. Any questions?"

"None, sir," I replied.

"Yes, one," said Pilgrim. "What's that great oak door at the foot of the granite cliff? It doesn't lead anywhere."

"That's right, Pilgrim," explained the voice. "It leads nowhere unless it pleases; the Answer Keeper is waiting for he who may open it and allow the light to flood the depths of the Lower Level. And the one for whom it opens shall be known as the Answer Keeper's true successor who will lead us to triumph and who will sit upon the Answer Keeper's right hand."

"Wouldn't that be rather uncomfortable?" Pilgrim commented.

"Do you have any questions, Saffron Tinker?" asked Faithful Night, ignoring the simpleton.

"I have one question only," said Saffron Tinker. "Is it due to my maturity of years or rather the sharpness of my eyesight that I've been promoted to Answer Keeper's Mules instead of being sent off to some cave as an apprentice flyer? And by the way, when can I go back to Támé Ingráleat at Stone Hollow?"

"That is more than one question," said Faithful Night.

"I never said I was good at counting."

"Well," considered the voice for a while, "there were other considerations regarding your 'promotion', and you may go to Stone Hollow when you have completed your service to Small Country. Now, if you will excuse me, I have a report to prepare. Farewell, would-be heroes, and goodbye."

Testimony Six

Prince Grind Underfoot is a hard master for those under his thumb but now that we were answerable only to Faithful Night and Mandrake Moon we didn't have to worry any more about that spiteful midget. He would get his orders from the Lower Level through the network screen, executing them to the letter and woe betide anyone that got in his way, he'd threaten to skin them alive that very afternoon. And by the end of that first week when war was declared, he had the town lockup chock-a-block with soldiers who'd got into his bad books somehow.

I can well remember Private Putt Upon from Slippery End getting three days straight in the block with no heat or blankets because he'd a button missing from his shirt. He would never have made it without the shirt Summer Willow slipped him, late one night, through the roof grating of his cell.

Then the new wire codes arrived. I thought no chance would these be cracked by the Heartless Bodies. I did know a thing or two about it, after all, having had a hand in the software development and all. Well, the day the new code arrives, Kills Two Birds from Frontier Province gets a month's hard drubbing from the cavedwarves for daring to suggest Small Country is now invincible.

"Just remember no one's bloody invincible!" shouted Grind Underfoot as the dwarves dragged him out of the hall.

"That's right!" said Pilgrim. "We've all gotta serve somebody!"

"What was that, you loathsome maggot?" screamed Grind Underfoot, stabbing a bony finger towards Pilgrim. "I'll make you sorry you said that, you sagging piece of pants elastic!"

"Don't speak to my deputy like that," I said, "or you'll have to answer to Faithful Night."

"You again!" he spluttered, grinding his teeth in a hissing fury. "When this war is over, you...!"

"Oh, and by the way, Grind Underfoot, about those units you claim we owe, we gave them to Mandrake Moon to buy spare parts for his Peace Apparatus, I'm sure you agree we did the right thing. And before I forget, Pilgrim World would like his special stones back now, please. You know, the ones you borrowed from him. Otherwise I'll tell Faithful Night you stole them."

Grind Underfoot's face went from red to purple to white as he sat on his throne crushing a golden cushion in his fists until the feathers flew like snow. But Pilgrim got his stones back and he stood there smiling as he counted them carefully into his sack.

"Gosh, thanks, Gwern," he said. "No one's ever been so kind to me before."

"Well you must have had it pretty rough then, that's all I can say; now shut it and let's go find Saffron Tinker to tell him we're off."

It didn't take us long to find Saffron Tinker; he was in his hut above the village, a pipe in his mouth, keeping an eye on the mules that grazed all over the hillside. The sun was gilding the reeds; the bracken was blood red. Birds chirped from the woods and New Village was like quarry rocks just fallen with the dust still rising. Saffron Tinker seemed to have landed on his feet up here, all he had to do was sit in his hut taking a suck on his pipe then spitting a gob or two into the fire, maybe now and then keeping half an eye out for his mules through the open door. All that daydreaming all alone must have fixed the fuses short-circuiting his head, too. He seemed pretty sorted.

"Come in, friends, take a pew," he announced as our shadows fell across the open door. "Explain who you are and do you take sugar."

"We've come to say goodbye for now," I said. "Pilgrim World and I fly at midnight with the first raid on the Exile States."

"Mules not good enough for you anymore, then? And what do you know about flying, you lying bedbug? And why d'you have to drag poor wideyed Pilgrim World after you? Oh, you drive me crazy, both of you! I really do give up this time!"

"Calm down, Saffron Tinker," I said soothingly. "I used to be the best on the Virtual Flying Game at All Night Café back home, you know, and haven't we been trained up by Mandrake Moon, Air Marshal of Answer Keeper's Air Peaceforce? He's taught us all he knows about the business, and these new systems are a piece of piss compared to the ones I'm used to."

"And if Gwern is going, I'm going too!" piped up Pilgrim defiantly. "He'll look after me, he will, you know, better than you ever did, you old duffer, you've only ever been cross and nasty to me and I..."

"Oh, listen to the monkey jabbering, listen to the lapdog biting back, you sly little whippersnapper, I'll show you...!"

"Be quiet both of you," I said, coming between them as Saffron Tinker slavered like a toad and Pilgrim tried to crawl under the table away from him. "Wise up, Saffron Tinker! And you stop winding him up, Pilgrim, look, you've got him going like a yo-yo! We'd better go. Thanks for the tea..."

"Yes, bugger off! Leave me here on my own then! See if I care. You little beggers leave me all alone on my mountain with no one but the wind for company months on end and then you turn up for five minutes and off again to your deaths in the Exile States and what am I supposed to do then? But what do you care, all stripes and style in your slick uniforms and your peaked caps, much good your fancy stripes will do you when you're lying in a ditch with crows pecking out your eyes and ngwaa ngwaa ngwaa aaa nngg..."

We could hear his voice shouting as we walked away under the flecked stars opening above us but the wind took away his words, thank God, and spat them out scornfully against the high crags. When I turned to look back all I could see was a dark spot by the hut darting back and forth like a spider sewing up his prey. I pulled my cap down hard on my head and with Pilgrim World following struck out back towards New Village.

We had to be at the air caves by eight, and we only just made it. Network codes tapped into the touchpad outside, slate slab door sliding noiselessly open, in we went to the preparation chamber. The other crews were already there, all paired up, crowding around the network screens for any last minute details.

"How's it going, lads?" called Boldbrass the Pilot, raising his head from his screen for a moment. "Ready to whip some ass?"

"The cat o'nine is ready and waiting," I called back. Just then Mandrake Moon strode into the chamber to deliver his pep spiel before we climbed into our machines. I didn't pay much attention to his speech because I'd heard it all before, drivelling on about his exploits in the first war and about the commemorative mural in Grind Underfoot's hall, the one with him slaying all those Heartless Bodies, how it was much bigger than anyone else's picture. On he droned about us young peace pilots having it real easy nowadays, the way we got to fly out to our deaths straight off without any of the strife the pilots of his day went through to get themselves slaughtered, those were the days. And those guards of Grind Underfoot's, no metal at all, waste of space. No two ways about it, without Mandrake Moon and his peace pilots, Small Country would be a pile of rubble and Faithful Night would be singing for his supper and so on and so forth ad infinitum. I was just itching to get going and aching to climb into my glove of a cockpit before anyone noticed my shaking hands. In the end he shut his trap and came amongst us doing the shaking hands and shoulder squeezing routine, wishing us each in turn good luck and filling our nostrils with his whisky-soaked breath. It was only then that they actually let us get on with the job in hand. Pilgrim World and I went to our peace machine and quickly checked her over, testing the jet stream indicators, adjusting the blades, making sure all circuits were open. Then up we went into the cockpit, masks and helmets wired and ready then thumbs up to the machine crews lined up to left and right. At the signal I powered up to the tenth level as the air gates opened slowly, surely and one by one the heavy-bellied machines rolled in sequence towards the take off line, their short wings springing out on either side and at the green light they roared away through the air gates, the heat of their jets warm on our faces even through our screens and visors. Seconds later all that was left of each would be a tiny shooting star, red-arsed, burnt out and fading into nothing.

"Appliance seven two one seven, Gwern Excuses, thirty seconds, over." The coordinator's voice broke in, "Line thirty, position for take off."

"Pilgrim," I commanded, "set the power compass to zero nought zero and confirm."

"Confirmed."

I threw the lock switch to release the wheels and slowly we rolled down along line thirty towards the air gates.

"Five, four, three, two, one, hit it!" said the coordinator. So I hit it and the engines roared as I locked the controls for take off and an unseen hand pressed us into our seats as the outside dissolved into strands and vanished behind us leaving only the night opening like a flower around us and the nose of our machine straining forwards towards the stars.

All the while the coordinator's voice kept up a commentary in our helmets, directing the fleet and confirming cross-references. Having drawn our wheels into the machine's underbelly all we had to do was sit and watch the red and green buttons of light flashing before us on the air screen, indicating that all was ticking over like clockwork.

"Appliance seven two one seven, confirm location," said the coordinator. I turned to Pilgrim.

"Ten over a hundred, seven seven eight south south east at three thousand units," said Pilgrim, reading off his power compass.

"Terminating voice contact," said the coordinator. "Dump on them, lads and safe home!" and we were all on our own with only the air screens to show us where we were within the fleet formation.

"Good lad," I said to Pilgrim. "You've learnt your lessons well."

"Thanks," said he. "I'm not afraid, mind. I trust you to bring us back home safely."

"Yes, relax, man. I'll buy you a slap up breakfast at Leather Belly's place tomorrow morning."

"Only thing is, though," Pilgrim added thoughtfully. "These missiles, they won't half mess up the Exile States, will they?"

"If we do our job properly, I guess they will, yes."

"And kill?"

"Military targets only, Pilgrim, nothing else."

"Yes, but..."

"Listen, Pilgrim, this is war: someone has to get killed or it wouldn't be a war at all, would it?"

"They'll die without knowing who killed them and we'll have killed them not knowing who we killed."

"It could happen, Pilgrim World old son. It wouldn't be the first time."

We stayed quiet for a long time after that as the machine thrust us further and further into the night until we noticed a narrow band of pink beginning to stain the clouds on the edge of the world down below.

I fixed back on the screens, checking the programmes were doing their stuff, and ran through the preliminary check list before arming the exit ports while we began to turn the machine slowly downwards towards the pink clouds to the right of us and the air screen flashed up: "Armed: Confirm".

That done we read the screen's assurance that the missiles were locked onto their targets.

"Missile One. Away," flashed the screen. I punched in the code and away it sailed in front of us, swerving to the left and then plunging into the clouds.

"Missile Two. Away," flashed the screen; this time it swerved away to our right.

The screens followed the missiles' flight path, showing the familiar cross-wires coming together to form a cross over some sort of factory buildings looming clearer and larger until they filled the screen.

"Missile One. Confirm target," flashed the screen. As I hit the red button the two wires parted directly above the buildings which imploded, pulverised, and spewed a ball of smoke like an egg yolk falling into a bowl of flour. Now on the other screen the two wires were poised over a lake or reservoir or somesuch and the cross came together over it.

"Missile two. Confirm target." I confirmed and watched as the screen zoomed in on the embankment where men were spilling like ants from hot water, out of their huts and scrambling along the dam wall. In a second the dam burst and a great wall of water and timber and rocks swept everything in its path taking the ants along with it and the screen closed with the message: "Accomplished".

"Back home then, I suppose." I turned to Pilgrim, a dull weight settling on my stomach as I thought of the ants being swept away.

"Is it all over?" asked Pilgrim, opening his eyes. All I could see through his visor were his shining, frightened eyes.

"Set the power compass for home, Pilgrim," I said, hearing the weariness grate in my voice.

"Home? Where is that?" he asked.

"Don't you start," I exclaimed angrily. "Bugger all help you've been so far when there was a bloody job to be done!"

"That's not what you said last night."

"Well it's a new day today. And you're no good to anyone: a fart in a bloody hurricane!"

All Pilgrim World did was stare out of his window, quiet, so I did the same and we let the machine take us on auto. That was when I saw the little glowing ball rising from the clouds towards us and before I'd a chance to activate the defence screen it had stuck fast to our right wing over my shoulder.

"Oh, Holy Shit," I said, wildly punching buttons on the pad in front of me and then came the splintering crack which shook us like puppets as I turned to see half my wing torn away with our second jet engine leaving us spiralling down through ragged broken clouds before hurtling towards an open picture book of fields and woods and hills and beyond a red desert crushed by the sun as my head burst and my ears screamed and the world turned around and around. Somehow I managed to scream through the mike as I fought to raise a hand or foot, "Hit the red button, Pilgrim, get out," while my stomach locked inside of me and through my seared eyes, through my red eyelids I saw snowflecked peaks glisten under a glinting sun and naked branches strewn with the raucous crows at Helen's Stone and the orchard trees all felled with their tangled twigs strangling the cart track where the orange and brittle bracken filled the ditches and the river choked on rusting machinery and rotting sheep, their fleece unwinding in the current, their teeth grimacing, their sockets open holes, and beyond, the whitewashed walls of Helen's Stone now streaked with black soot, the roof fallen and the windows shattered, the smell of damp soot on the air and its colour bleeding on the wet washing still hanging on the line, the front door creaking on one hinge, no sign of life. I fell upon my knees and closed my eyes. Tight, tight to shut it out and I began to turn in a starless night longing only for your arms around me and no lies between us.

Daylight was what I got, bursting all around me as I span sickeningly through whistling space, and the rush and tear of canvas and a snapping jolt and there I was swinging, sitting, slowly turning in my ejector seat gently sinking in the hanging shadow of a parachute's umbrella. First thing I saw were the red hills rising on my left so I guided the seat towards them using the steering buttons on its arms. Good job I did too because I'm sure the Heartless Bodies were crawling around the other side of those hills where the machine must have gone down, waiting there for me to land. But there I was, floating gently down, alive and not a crack of enemy fire on the air, only my ragged thoughts, "Where's that Pilgrim World got to?" Turn up in a moment, probably…." Then I noticed a weight pressing down on my lap and saw Pilgrim's sack of stones sitting there with its neck tucked neatly under my seat belt. I stared unblinking at it.

"Poor Pilgrim," I said eventually, out loud; over and again his name echoed all around me. All the while the ground was getting closer, the seat was drifting in the rising air currents; I had to concentrate on landing my contraption which was easier said than done. The marsh was soft at least when we hit the ground, but shit it wasn't us at all was it, it was me, alone. Alone for the first time I couldn't think straight in the silence; my thoughts wound back to Pilgrim World and his little set of stones. I thought of him being beaten by Grind Underfoot and me standing up for him. I bit my lip as I thought of him lying in pieces in some ditch with ants a black dust over him. "Why didn't you do as I told you and get out, Pilgrim? Why did you press my button first…." I looked around me at the swamp and the red foothills to the desert beyond; vultures were circling above. "What would you do in a place like this, Pilgrim?" I thought, and imagined his answer: "Well, I'd be with you, Gwern." I unclipped myself from the seat and pushing it to one side, struggled through the swamp and towards the brittle red hills.

Can I skip the bit about the treck from the swamp to the hills? It's a long story and my backup batteries are low. All you need to know is it took weeks that felt like months. Travelling by night in enemy territory at the white hot heart of war by all accounts, lost deep in the Exile States. Actually not quite the heart as it turned out; I'd ended up on the margins where the desert fades into the barren red hills and they in turn give way to forested ranges garlanded with waterfalls. My feet and legs were swollen by the time I arrived in the temperate zone where I was voted meal of the day by the local leeches; they'd drop from trees on your sleeping head and slurp up your blood without even bothering to wake you. Only keeping on thinking about Pilgrim kept me going, gave me steel to live. At long last I reached a hermit's hut in a hollow where the water shatters as it falls on his creaking water wheel. I could jabber enough Exilespeak to conceal my Lowland accent and I made up some sob story that seemed to do the trick. He fed me egg on toast and I gave him my flying suit in exchange for some peasant clothes. The hermit hadn't even heard of the war; hadn't even heard of Small Country, bless him, and neither had his white cat.

He turned out to be a bit of a preacherman. I became his regular late-night audience of one for his repenting sessions.

"You are a great sinner!" he goes, jabbing a gnarled finger into my chest.

"I know. Don't rub it in," I agreed. How come news of me had travelled so fast?

"I too am a great sinner!" he cried, beating himself on his breast. "I am the greatest sinner the world has ever known!"

"Is that why you've got to live out here with no one to visit you?"

"Of the seven deadly sins I have committed eight," he continued. "Whenever I feel myself moving closer to God, God moves away from me as if my breath stinks. My cat Pangur Bán, now, she's saintly compared to me, even if she is a hopeless mouser."

"What exactly did you do to deserve all this?" I asked, hoping to winkle out a few nuggets on the Exile States' legal system.

"Do?" he seemed miffed. "I didn't do anything. It was my thoughts that were impure. That's the very worst sin of all. Do you?"

"Do I what?"

"Think impure thoughts?"

"Get away from me you pervert!" I shouted, casting off his clutches.

"You must punish me tomorrow," he said. "It's late. Come to bed."

"I'll be fine in the shed, hermit," I said and I was out there like a shot and locked myself in with a floor brush wedged inside the door.

It was best all round that I left early next day before the hermit woke and the Heartless Bodies picked up my trail and got me tortured and killed. Anyway I had other plans. Actually I made quite a fine Exile peasant, though I say so myself. It was easy going, tramping their countryside like a beggar, dodging stray missiles like a native. I felt no hatred of the people, but I kept my distance in case someone should see through my disguise. Sometimes I'd just act dim and that way bluffed my way out of a fair few sticky situations.

I wound up sheltering in Schadenfreude Forest, in a hay loft some old forester had near the village weir of some place, don't ask me how you pronounce its name. In return for food and shelter I carried grain to the local mill. The old forester's daughter was a nice girl and the old forester's wife treated me just fine and everything was hunky dory, so I got to thinking maybe I could stay there for a while and forget all about Small Country and Pilgrim, forget about Lowland and perhaps even you, Little Caress Heart, thinking I'd go native, turn myself into a proper Exile like Ivan Echo from Betws who went to work as a ticket collector on Rausman Central all those years ago, I was just thinking all that when who d'you think arrived to shoot the whole damn dream to pieces? Saffron Tinker and his bloody mules.

I'm in the farmyard shovelling manure from a wheelbarrow onto the dung heap when he shows up from nowhere, his pack of mules, filling the yard.

"Are you mad?" I cried. "Come round the other side of the cowshed, you idiot." I was petrified we'd be seen together. "And get these animals to come with you!"

"Things aren't so great, not so very good either," said Saffron Tinker. "No more Pilgrim. No more Gwern Excuses. Not too good. Not too splendid at all."

"What are you drivelling on about, you warped wombat? Don't talk like that. Look, it's me, Gwern! But they don't know that around here, just call me Hau'ab Schmutztuck while you're here."

"Is it really you, Hau'ab Schmutztuck?" cried Saffron Tinker, leaping from his mule. "Where is Pilgrim, is he around?"

"No, he's history."

"And they let you live...? Listen, I'm here disguised as a sane man come to rescue you both. One will never do! Come on, climb on a mule and we'll go look for him."

"How many mules did you bring?"

"Enough. Come on."

"Actually I was having a good time here until you came," I replied, miffed at his attitude.

"You want to bury yourself in this hole until you rot, is that it? You think you can hide your head in that dung heap, do you? Fine then, you just nuzzle down here, shit sheriff. But you won't hide from your fate."

"I can try though."

"I'll be mad if you don't come. Just choose a mule!"

"Not the mad bit, anything but that," I said sadly. "I'll take the brown one."

"What's all this noise?" shouted the old forester, striding towards us.

"Ah! And a good morning to you again too!" I said. "Ehm, my friend Bettenhauen here was just reminding me that I've an appointment with him today in Entwürdigung City. I've been so busy shovelling dung I clean forgot about it. I shall see you tonight, and don't worry, I'll shovel all night to make up for this afternoon."

"Entwürdigung City? Gosh, you will make it there and back in an afternoon d'you reckon?"

"No problem," said Saffron Tinker. "Look at the mules we've got."

"Strange accent," said the old forester.

"It's Schopfer Wohlgefallt's accent, actually," said Saffron Tinker. "I borrowed it while he's on holiday. Come on, Hau'ab Schmutztuck, we can't stand around here gossiping all day."

Testimony Seven

All Saffron Tinker wanted to talk about was the war effort, how badly things would seem to go one minute but the next they'd pronounce a new dawn that would usher in a rosier era. The length of each era had been curtailed to a quarter of an hour, he said, to economise on gossip. Great Vineyard had pulled out at the last minute in favour of a better offer elsewhere and Bhaarata hadn't even bothered to turn up. However Earth Vineyard and Long Island were shoulder to shoulder in the breach together with Small Country and Lowland, Sunless Summer, Wild Country and Bleak Winter.

"Quite some breach," I commented. "But I can't believe Bleak Winter has joined. Do you see those Swarthy Cavedwarves pulling their weight?"

"No, you're right, I'm sorry, actually they just pulled out too. But all the rest are in and we've really got a chance now."

"Have you been looking for us... I mean, me... long?"

"How long have you been missing?" was his reply. "Mind you, with my contacts," he continued, making me glad to hear him speak lucidly. "I could bake foxgloves before dawn."

"Come on now, Tinker, you were doing well there for a while."

"Don't pressurise me, Gwern. Kick that mule and hurry. It's easier if you get on to him before you kick him. Look, over that ridge there, below in the glen lying in wait is Fionn Trá regiment, Gonéirín Bóthar-Leat's finest infantrymen, or what's left of them."

"Are you sure?"

"Sure I'm sure. That's how I came here, stupid. They'll give us shelter and we can follow them back to Lowland where my Támé Íngráleat is waiting for me."

"You brought her to this place, screwball?"

"It's not so dangerous, what's wrong with you? Isn't this one of those new technology wars? How much 'collateral damage' did you see *chez* old forester and family?"

"None," I admitted. "Just on TV every night when they let me watch it; mostly they'd go wild cheering as our boys took a pasting."

"Peasants," said Saffron Tinker contemptuously, spitting out a long jet of brown tobacco juice all over his trouser leg. "Damn it, the wife'll kill me for that now." His mule muled on as he rubbed furiously at the stain with a dirty rag but pretty soon the white peaks of Gonéirín Bóthar-Leat's tents came into view over the rise and I paid him no more attention.

"War envoys of Faithful Night! Welcome!" cried Gonéirín Bóthar-Leat coming from his tent towards us. "Come inside to quench your thirst."

You'd have thought we were princes the welcome we got with the potsheen flowing and all the very best the camp kitchens could provide: potatoes.

"Go on, have another, just one more," urged Gonéirín Bóthar-Leat.

"Well, just one then," I said, trying to push another potato into my mouth, and doing the same for Saffron Tinker.

"Nngggww nggwww nggaaa," he spluttered in protest.

"I'm sorry about Pilgrim," said Gonéirín Bóthar-Leat when all the potatoes had gone. "Giving his life to save his master. Sure, you wouldn't get that nowadays, now, would you?"

"I'm sorry too," I snapped. "I didn't want him to save me. But he did it and it's over. What gets me is how mean I'd been to him and I never said I didn't mean it. But he forgave me anyway or I wouldn't be here now so you can shut it, Gonéirín Bóthar-Leat and mind your own business!"

"And it only happened a few months ago, you Long Island arsehole," shouted Saffron Tinker, beginning to froth at the mouth.

"Come, drink," said Gonéirín Bóthar-Leat without turning a

hair. "Throw it west lads, we'll get another in."

We made a big night of it, I remember that much. There we were still at it as the blue dawn filtered through the tent. He had explained the whole campaign strategy to us, using pictures, diagrams, sticking pins into maps and explaining in detail the exact reason we were being hammered. I just wish I could remember some of the things he told us. Saffron Tinker lost interest early on and began snoring from his wooden armchair. I was all ears listening to the exploits of the Fionn Trá Regiment shoulder to shoulder with Rock Jaw's bandit warriors and their Shining Beasts holding Sliabh Eoghann Pass for seven days and six nights until Befehlnotstand arrived in person leading reinforcements from Entwürdigung Castle and drove off the Alliance forces.

He told of Mandrake Moon's air raids and his missiles that hailed down out of a clear sky to keep the Exile States at bay. He said this was all that stood between us and the Heartless Bodies.

He told of Grind Underfoot as he led one hundred infantrymen with Captain White Fear and how, as they passed through Bleak Winter, they'd been hounded by the Ice Locusts and driven to despair by the Swarthy Cavedwarves. Grind Underfoot had failed to negotiate a settlement with them and been forced to return to Small Country in his vest and underpants with half his men lost over the precipice. Faithful Night had dismissed him and was looking for a new prince now.

"Hasn't he sent the word out far and wide," added Gonéirín Bóthar-Leat, "under the seal of the Answer Keeper, that he even wants you back to try the Door of Answers in case it might be you!" He seemed very amused by the thought.

"Well, I can't go," I boasted drunkenly. "I've got other irons in the fire."

Gonéirín Bóthar-Leat went off to bed and left me pondering over the dregs.

Just before dawn the regiment's horn sounded and I woke to see Saffron Tinker leap to his feet and smack his palm smartly to his temple, standing to attention like a soldier.

"I am a soldier now," he explained. "I've got the stripes to prove it. Think I'm kidding? Look, pull up the back of my shirt."

"How d'you get these?" I asked, rubbing my eyes.

"Stealing flour from Nabac Leish's stores back in the Valley of Forgetting before we got to the Exile States. I tell you it cleared my head though."

The lads were pulling down our tent around us, folding it about our ears and carrying Gonéirín Bóthar-Leat's bed to his cart and him sleeping like a baby nestled in its feathers.

"So much for your new-tech war," I croaked hoarsely to Saffron Tinker. "Not much sign of it so far in this bloody quagmire."

"Of course there's no evidence on the ground," he said patiently. "Perhaps you missed the only piece of substance to be grasped from all Gonéirín Bóthar-Leat's hot air last night? Head in the clouds, nothing but mist between the ears."

"Of course I got it," I replied grumpily. "I was just testing you. Energy sources used up, no power anymore, that's it, isn't it? But they've enough left up in Small Country or the peace machines couldn't still fly, obviously?"

"Not obvious to me," proclaimed Saffron Tinker as he loosened his mules' reins from the stake. "You can kiss goodbye to your peace machine, I'd say, and go buy some faster stripes for your mule. Sober up, will you, we're moving out!"

What an excruciating trip. Gonéirín Bóthar-Leat somehow had it in his head we were gentlemen and each night he would invite us to one of his 'soirees'. I suppose Saffron Tinker was technically nobility now, having married Prince Gonéirín Bóthar-Leat's sister and all. I guess he left out the bit about Mrs Saffron Tinker and his part in her downfall. I wasn't about to spill the beans either; Tinker didn't even know that I knew about his past.

As each new day dawned Gonéirín Bóthar-Leat would climb into bed to be carried along in his cart while I perched in pain on the back of my mule. As for Saffron Tinker, he'd happily adapted to his unique riding stile which he laughingly called "saddle" and for longer journeys, with arms and legs bound as a girth under the mule's belly, he would sleep away the day, dreaming his strange dreams.

We dragged along through the mud between high matted hedges of blackthorn and brambles, a long line of open-shirted Long Islandmen, wet clay sucking on their marching steps; behind them Gonéirín Bóthar-Leat's cart with his comfy camp bed wedged tight between its deep sides and him oblivious to the tossing and turning over pothole or rock.

Saffron Tinker slept off the night's excesses under his mule like a bushbaby, while I tried to sleep in the saddle and not fall off. The war band was completed by a rear-guard of Saffron Tinker's spare mules. We offered the lads one each but they wouldn't have it. Séd O'Bheatha from Cinéal Súgrach spoke for them all when he said: "Mules are for peasants; we are descended from Bhfuil Athas Ort. Keep your mules, we know how to walk."

Pathetic hillocks smutted with black soot spoiled the view all around us. The only cheering sight was the curls of smoke rising here and there from the pock-marked fields like corpse candles.

On we went, on and on. Gradually the hillocks began to fatten, as did the clouds filling slowly with rain, showers growing stronger daily until they tipped down on us like a water spout. We won't be long to Lowland now, I said when I noticed a snail on a leaf. The next creature I saw was a green frog then two little mice and after that three rats and above in the trees an old crow grown too weak for croaking.

"Tinker, Tinker, wake up!" I shouted, seeing my first sheep gnawing a tuft of grass. The bugger didn't stir.

Lowland was much the same as before but you could feel that there had been changes. I was just glad most of the fighting had been in more formidable places. The war is ever present here through the television, of course, and the people were wary until they knew you and where you came from. I'd long since shaken off the remnants of Fionn Trá Regiment, telling Saffron Tinker I'd look in on him and Támé Ingráleat at Stone Hollow when I got the chance. He took my hand as I turned to go: "I've a fine place there, kept a summer cottage over the winter and when you come, Támé Ingráleat'll make us tea the way we like it, with a good shot of whisky in it."

"Keep back a bottle for me then," I said and we shook on it.

The main change you noticed were the roads. Main roads without cars, only people on mule-back or on bikes. All energy points closed. Going rate: six cars equals one bike. For a mule you could get one bike and a good suit of clothes. That's what I got, anyway, after haggling. It was a huge black bicycle and the suit wouldn't have been out of place at chapel. Got a dirty look off the mule as I left him, into the bargain. Was sorry to lose a friend but round here you get more respect in a suit on a bike than in a sack on a mule. So off I went, pedal-pace along the country lanes, an unknown Lowlander in his Sunday best, the only response from those I met a courteous "Nice morning" and "Going far?"

It was a change not to feel frightened. I could never ease up in the Exile States, even when I was staying with the old forester. Now at last I could breathe again, free to go as I pleased, incognito in my tidy suit.

I was looking down on Town Square from the fields. I guess I know every bush, every thicket within two miles. I knew Redbeak's barn in the High Pasture was a good place to sleep, he would never call his cows for milking until after the ten o'clock freedom call next morning, so that's where I spent the night. His haybarn is a total mess, what with the rain seeping in like hourglass sand, spoiling the hay. "I should have stayed in Sam Stammer's old barn at Cold Hillside," I decided. "At least he's got a tidy farm."

What did I look like at first light, trundling my bike down the lane? The clouds were crumbling and stars were going out;

chaffinches sounded in the trees, wrens' chirps mixed with the sound of other winter birds. I stroked my hand on moss like a furry caterpillar lining the walls; it was brittle with frost. There was no one around, no smoke from chimneys. The summits were waiting for sunrise's whitewash.

I hid the bike at Gorse Gable under a clump of dry bracken in a bank at the furthest tilled field-end and lit out on foot over the walls, across the fields.

By the time I reached the gate to Helen's Stone the snow shone bright on the summits through the lifting mists but the hazels of Helen's Stone were bare and cold. Twigs snapped beneath my feet; crows cawed crossly, drawn from sleep by my passing. Then I saw the orchard trees on their sides across the path. My feet like eggshell crunching on the stiff tall grass, the river gurgling, choking with strewn carcases of furniture, bits of old machines, leafmould and a dead sheep, the fleece unwinding from her body, her frozen smile gaping like her black eyeless sockets. I ran, stumbling past the bend in the path to Helen's Stone. "Caress," I called as I pushed open the door hanging on one hinge. I saw on whitewashed walls the stain of black slime belched from windows, the rafters like the ribs of a boat. Soot rustled as it slid now and then from the crossbeams, its colour leached into the limp sheets hanging like thieves on the line. I shouted "Caress!" again but only the crows laughed out an answer.

Why couldn't I just fall to my knees and dig my fingers into the wet ground, cursing the day I set off from home? Instead I stepped, soot trickling down my neck, into the dying shell.

I knew where to look. The note was fixed next to the hearthstone. "Waiting for you in Entwürdigung Castle. Caress."

"Think I'm gonna fall for that one, do you?" I spat, knowing that spidery hand straight off. "Scarlet Nightshade, that snitching little bitch!"

At least I knew now. I just dragged a stick through the wreckage, picking up this and that from the ashes. I found a tiny boot, all scorched. I found your gold brooch, its pin was broken; a blackened photo of you and Calonnog, its frame charred and bent. Outside on a thorn bush some ragged pages fluttered and I saw your handwriting on one of them, all bleached by sun and rain. I kept the only page that was legible, its edges brittled and brown, and it is here now on the table at Stone Hollow, my candle lighting its yellowing paper:

...but its taste to me was honey.

There is a valley in my heart,
and all along it flows a river,
on its banks are trees and meadows
and an old hearth that lies in ruins.

If I could sit on its banks again
with you and me as we were before
this hearth would spring to life
and the world would not be cold.

One night storms came to this valley
and tore up the trees and holed our roof
with thunder and with rain
they split my heart in two....

I was thinking what Faithful Night had told me in his cave. Thinking what he would see in my heart now, Caress; would he see the same in both our hearts this time? I took another look at that ruined cottage and I felt my heart knot tight against those that did all this to us.

By the time I got back to my bike there were people about, but they didn't see me. I went down Hendre Hill, on the road to Stone Hollow, and with the wind behind me it didn't take long. I shouted, "Anyone here?" before pushing open the door to catch

Saffron Tinker in frilly apron making breakfast for Mrs Támé Ingráleat-Saffron.

"Hello, Gwern," he said as if I'd hardly left his side.

"Where's my breakfast, Saffron Tinker?" shouted the Princess from the bedroom.

"I'm making breakfast for three now, precious flower. Gwern Excuses has arrived."

"Well, a thousand welcomes, my beauty," she shouted, bounding from the bedroom and planting a resounding kiss on my cheek.

"You'll never get that lipstick off, you know," was Saffron Tinker's dejected response.

"Shut up and bring us coffee, you big lout," she commanded as she swung onto the bench and started giving me the third degree.

I don't mind being questioned by someone I trust. It was funny, because I'd only spoken with her once before, in Bás le Tart's pub in the Town of the Wattle Fords... But it felt like I did know her after all and I liked the way she looked into the mess in my heart and did not turn away. "There, now, treasure. Don't take all the blame on your two shoulders. Look at me and Saffron Tinker here, now he deserves all the blame he can get, of course." Saffron Tinker took no notice, he just carried on grilling oysters, the hot fat spattering his nose. She suffers no fools, least of all him. He knew that already, though, or he wouldn't have married her, I suppose.

Saffron Tinker is pretty as a picture in his frilly apron, pirouetting across the floor with a plateful of breakfast in each hand, singing old ballards, his purple nose shining bright.

"I'm much better now, thank you, Princess Támé Ingráleat-Saffron," I said.

"Call me Tá, sweetie, it's less formal," she replied, pouring me out another cup.

Staying with the Saffrons did me the world of good, no doubt about it. My thoughts never got stuck on the same old track with her around to derail them.

"You'll be heading out for Rausman's castle soon, will you?" she asked one fine morning, placing her coffee cup carefully on its saucer. "Entwürdigung Castle is a daunting place my precious, have you ever been there?"

"Not really," I said.

She got maps and charts, saying: "If you're going to go, go now!" She raised her cup to her lips. "And take my blessings with you, sweetie. Safe journey!"

What could I do but wave at them, seeing me off by the garden gate? The bicycle wobbled, I pushed at the pedals, we were on our way.

I was lost somewhere in the Exile States trying to find the old forester's cottage: the maps I had were of someplace else. Space gypsies from Under Milk Sun saved me, if you believe some of the stories. Others, closer to the truth tell of elbow grease, pedal power and a dash of cunning. I kept my head down through central Exile States, and in the end I found my old aquaintance. "Had a wonderful few days in Entwürdigung City; marvellous place," I told the forester when he asked me where the hell I'd got the bicycle. "Hundreds of them there," I went on, getting into my stride. "The place is crawling with them. You've never seen so many bicicles! They're all filthy rich there, for Christ's sake, you've never seen anything like it. Just look what passes for rubbish in their gutters," I said showing him one of Pilgrim's red stones from his old sack. The old forester opened his eyes wide in wonder as though he might swallow it. "Take it," I said. "I don't know what it's worth around here. Dirt cheap where I come from."

"Gentle sir!" cried the old forester. "You're an Entwürdigung City gentleman, sir, I can tell! Oh joyous morning!"

"And it's taken you all this time to notice?" I said in a rather tired tone. "Why has it taken you so long to find out? By the way, what is your name, for the record?"

"Old Forester, sir. And here is the wife, sir, she would like to kiss the shoes you were born in, sir."

"And is she called Wife of Old Forester, by any chance?" I asked.

"Yes, sir, she is," said the Old Forester. "I wish I could have gone to college and become an intellectual like you, sir."

"Are you taking the piss or are you just thick?" I demanded. "Anyway you didn't and you aren't," I spat crossly as I'd seen the Exile States nobility treat their inferiors. "And by the way, I'm appropriating the contents of your miserable hovel in the name of Rausman our Great Leader as well as everything else you may have of any value plus any land a narrow shot from your door."

"Begging your pardon, 'an arrow shot', sir."

"When I want your opinion, serf, I'll look for it down the toilet, you buffoon. Get out of my sight, load the cart with your stuff and get ready to leave!"

"*Ja vol!*" said Old Forester, thrilled to his fingertips, almost striking out his eye with his forefinger, so smart was his salute. Too smart, in fact: had he got me sussed? "No," I decided, "I've got this arsehole eating out of my hand."

"*Ja vol!*" I replied but the noise my felt heels made together was a soft sorry excuse for the shiny black clip effect I was aiming for.

"Get out your best high boots, Forester, and while you're at it bring me the family's best suit as well. Not one that makes me look like a Methodist minister, I've done that one; dress me as a military man with a literary bent for my re-entry into Entwürdigung City!"

Wife of Old Forester turned out handy with a needle: a few fine stitches and who'd doubt but that this was the uniform of the Buchhalter Kommando rank. I took a goose quill from the old codger's hat and I took the only book they had in the house, unwrapped it from its greaseproof paper and in no time I looked the spitting image of a Buchhalter Kommando official.

"And listen," I hissed, my new importance puffing out against my brass buttons, "the girl can stay here to tend the land and guard the swag, I mean keep watch over this property owned exclusively by Rausman our Great Leader." I thought for a bit and then added, "We shouldn't be wasting energy in this thrifty age, so I'll just pull the plug...." The network screen went blank and then I cut the wire. I didn't want news of our journey to travel before us, now did I?

Testimony Eight

As it turned out Old Forester and Old Forester's Wife were good at pulling bikes. After all, an officer of the Buchhalter Kommando would not be seen dead pedalling his own bicycle.

They swallowed my story of being on mission for Rausman; the way the details changed from time to time was just part and parcel of my mystique. My identity as an official remained unchanged, unlike the purpose of our mission or the facts surrounding our arrival: we passed ourselves off as natives of Zigenner City, Heerschau City and even Schadenfreude Forest.

Entwürdigung Castle was perched on its hilltop with the Häfling River wound like a sleepy snake round its base and the city all around it. Saffron Tinker had told me about the kites with three metre wingspans wheeling above the castle towers: I'd thought he was having me on. I bet they feed them with the bodies of Lowland prisoners, or how else would they be so tame? Swooping close as shadows past the watchmen's shoulders as they dive plumb from the ramparts.

"Begging your pardon, sir," Old Forester asked, "but what time is the appointment with Rausman our Great Leader?" The name inspired awe and terror in him and he gave a salute.

"Never you mind about that," I replied with authority. "I've decided to see him tomorrow and will therefore require overnight lodgings. No budget stuff, mind. The works!"

Old Forester went off to find somewhere while his wife, the bike and I ended up in a nearby tavern, all in aid of soaking up some local atmosphere. Unfortunately there wasn't any. At the bar I heard someone say, "What was the United score tonight?"

Someone else accused him of being a plonker and said next time he parked next to him could he leave him a tin-opener so he could get back in. Things started to look up when a really smart girl came up to the bar next to me. She got her fancy cocktail and then asked for a card for the cigarette machine, handing over a fifty unit bill. "Now then," I thought to myself, "here's where the skeletons come dancing out of the closets."

"Machine on stairs there," shouted the proprietor. "Nowt left but tens of Mellow Sidney."

"That's not very patriotic," snapped back the girl, snatching the cigarette card from his hand.

"What I mean to say is," he spluttered, "that it is my honour to announce that I have available, through the bountiful generosity and unflinching bravery of Rausman our Great Leader, plenty of tens of Mellow Sidney."

"That's better," said she as she took the fags from him.

She went to sit in a window seat and looked at no one while she smoked. No one looked at her directly. Christ, I've seen livelier funerals. I told the landlord that given who we were, we did not pay for drinks. I showed him my badge and made him sign my register. I told him he was lucky he'd not been closed right down, that he mind his tongue in future when it came to seditious talk about cigarette stocks. I was crawling the walls with boredom by the time Old Forester got back.

"Where the bloody hell have you been?" I demanded.

"I've been arranging lodgings," said Old Forester.

I asked him to show me, and on arriving asked, "You call these lodgings?"

"It says Providence Peace House above the door: maybe they'll provide a bit of peace, eh, sir," he replied. "A bed and breakfast only, but on a night like this..."

"Shut up," I said. "Have you got us rooms?"

"Humbly report, sir," said Old Forester, "my orders were to find the place sir, that was all."

"You what?" I screamed, his dozy flummery driving me crazy. "And stop calling me 'sir', you cretin. From now on address me only as 'Your Highness'. And this is not a lodging house, it's a bloody manse! Oh what's the use, just knock on the door, see what happens."

"They'll be Church of Rausman," said Old Forester, knocking loudly. "That's what they all are round here nowadays. Lovely religion, mind. Kind as anything. Would give you the shirt off their back unless it was worth anything. As you know, I myself remain true to the way of Shri Rupaiah who came down in a wheel of fire with six swirling swords in his hands, sweeping all from his path."

"Have you been drinking, Old Forester?"

"Chest a trop, to boozt the old blood sugar," he answered as the door opened and a spectacularly unamused citizen viewed us from his threshold.

"What the hell is the meaning of this commotion?" he demanded.

"Grand Officer Hau'ab Schmutztuck of the Buchhalter Kommando is the meaning of this commotion, citizen," I said coldly, clicking heels and raising my forefinger to my eye. "Show me your papers."

"Ernst Gewalt at your service," he replied, fishing them from his dressing gown pocket. "Network code: eleven, forty one, thirty nine. Occupation: Capo, stone dressers' section, City Embellishment. The books are open on my desk upstairs. But come, come inside; my wife will be delighted to get up to make you a bite to eat."

"A bite to eat?" I said. "That will not do at all. Go and wake the butcher, get some of that venison, it's in season now. Get something suitable from the wine shop too while you're at it, I'm rather thirsty."

"*Ja vol!*" said our host.

"And not a word to anyone," I added, tapping my nose. "Confidential."

"*Ja vol!*" he repeated and rushed off into the night.

"Why not lay the table, Citizenne Gewalt," I said to his wife who was standing to attention. That's how officers of my rank address people in the Exile States. Old Forester and his wife took to the rough way I treated them like suky lambs to the bottle. Ok, so maybe it looks like I was getting a real stuck up arrogant brute, but no way would they have respected me if I hadn't treated them mean. After a while it had actually started to come natural to me; after a bit I felt like Grind Underfoot at the peak of his powers. But I wouldn't fall from grace like he did, not here in the Exile States, no sir. Anyway Citizenne Gewalt was glad to follow my suggestion. Soon the provisions had been brought and the meal prepared.

"Citizen Gewalt," I said, leaning back in my chair, the venison, red wine and fine spirits all tucked away nicely under my belt. My two peasants were already bedded down in the under-stair cupboard for the night. "Citizen Gewalt," I said, "let's put you to the test. What did you say your work was?"

"Capo in the stone dressers' department, City Embellishment, Your Highness."

"No need to be formal," I told him. "You can just call me 'sir'." He made a bow. "City Embellishment, is it? And how far over budget are you with the work in hand?"

"You mean the tower? A couple of million units, rising."

"I see you're no mean estimator," I replied. "Unforeseen circumstances, no doubt?"

"Oh, yes, sir! Nothing seems to satisfy her. She's not like us here, content to sketch a black and white box and live in that, no, sir, not her. She wants windows that open outwards and then once they're in she wants them opening inwards instead. The doors were worse. Whoever heard of a door hinged to the floor? Well she had to try it, didn't she, wouldn't listen to my argument that the whole point of a door is to offer a way through a wall without actually knocking it down."

"That's the way it is with these strangers," I agreed, pricking up my ears. "So many foreign prisoners around nowadays, aren't there?"

"Indeed there are; too many by far. They get all the best food while we go without... what I mean is, they're well looked after but not as well as us citizens, living off the fat of the land. But that girl, she'll eat nothing but what takes her fancy, and that's not much, so the cook Ungesttalten told me. I said she was just as fussy about the interior design of her cell."

"Women!"

"And that brat of a boy she's got, making sandcastles in our cement sand and messing it up, running wild all over the place like a billy goat. It shouldn't be allowed."

"I see, well, very interesting. I do hope you fully appreciate the honour of this official visit?"

"Indeed I do, sir!" Our host bowed low, sweeping the knuckles of one hand over his boot.

"I'm going to bed, now, Citizen Gewalt. Good night."

"Good night, sir," said Ernst Gewalt.

"Good night, your Highness," said Citizenne Gewalt. "When would you like your morning repast?"

"When I wake up," I yawned from the stairs.

We walked in the thick of the castle's deep shadow the following morning as I accompanied Citizen Ernst Gewalt to inspect the accounts he'd left at work.

"You know you shouldn't leave official papers at work," I scolded him. "Otherwise how can you carry on working when you get home?"

"I'm sorry, sir," he apologised. "Come, sir, this way. Simply enter your network code into the keypad and in we go."

"I know all about that," I said dryly. "If I enter my network code it'll get out that I'm here and my secret mission on behalf of Rausman our Great Leader won't be so secret any more, will it? What's your network code again, Citizen Gewalt?"

"Eleven, forty one, thirty nine, sir. Am I still allowed to call you 'sir', your Highness?"

"Yes, yes," I said as the green light came on. "Now get out of my way. I'll go alone today, incognito. However, tomorrow, do you know what I'll do for you?"

"I do not, sir."

"I will let you enter using my network code and I will introduce you to Rausman our Great Leader himself! I'll see you at dinner time."

"Oh, thank you, sir! What an honour, sir. Your dinner will be ready upon your return."

In I went, walking tall along wide corridors as though I knew the place like the back of my hand and was in a hurry to reach my appointment. I wasn't the only one. There were hundreds just like me, everyone rushing around clutching armfuls of papers to their chests to the clacking of manual typewriters from the offices which lined the long passages. "I can't run around like this forever like a dog chasing its tail," I said to myself, by now quite lost in the honeycomb maze of corridors, stairways, lobbies and offices. "This is even worse than that Emperor Bara Hathi's place and that was bad enough."

I put my head around the door of the next office I passed, causing all the secretaries to look up. They immediately stood up to attention when they saw my rank, making the Exile States' salute with their index fingers.

"Your Most Excellent Highness," they said in unison. "The bar is on the next floor."

"I'm not looking for the bar," I retorted, drawing my leather gloves through my hands. "I'm being misdirected at every turn here as I try to bring my mission to a successful conclusion. I was advised that this was the Repair and Renewal Department Office."

"Everyone makes the same mistake, sir," chirped up a cheeky young blonde – I soon found that informality was the rule amongst the office girls, very few seemed to address their superiors as they should, but as no one seemed to notice I put up with it. "No one can find anything here, sir, since Security took down the direction screens from all the lobbies."

"Of course security considerations are paramount, girls."

"Yes, sir, how right you are, sir," she cried. "Now, sir, Repair and Renewal is part of Bettnachzieher's office and it's seventeen floors up, the stairs are first left at the end of the next right hand corridor."

"I'm pleased to note that you do not suggest using the lift."

"Oh, no, sir! We're all for this new energy conservation drive. Save it, sir, every time! Anyway, it never wor... ehm, actually, sir, we've been saving energy on it since the day it was installed."

"Well, girls, I must not keep you from your duties. Your patriotic enthusiasm will be noted in my report." My tongue was wearying from wrestling with all those Exile States consonants and I was glad to push on.

All a lather I finally reached the right floor so I leant against a wall to catch my breath before knocking at Bettnachzieher's door.

"Come," said his secretary's voice.

"And a good day to you too," I said, stepping in.

"He's out on business. You'll have to wait. No idea when he'll be back. Take the armchair over there. Tea or coffee?"

"Is Bettnachzieher often out during office hours?" I inquired from the chair as I sipped my black coffee.

"I wouldn't like to say, sir."

"Would you like to go straight to jail, my girl?"

"I would not, sir. He's out more than he's in. I used to say that he'd gone to the toilet but he didn't like that. 'If I'm out I'm out on business,' he'd say. 'Don't say I've gone to the toilet or that I haven't got up yet, there's a good girl.'"

"Well, I'm afraid this cannot wait any longer. In confidence, my visit concerns the new tower. Shenanigans to do with the accounts."

"Oh, you're the one they've sent to sort it all out, sir? High time too if you ask me. What a scandal! Do you know the price they've been paying for cement? You could build a palace for what that tower's cost and it's not even close to being finished!"

"You've not mentioned this to anyone else?" I asked. "This is a delicate situation and some discretion would be appropriate, do you understand?"

"But the story's all over the castle, sir. Thank God you're here to put a stop to it all, sir."

"Yes, yes, I know," I muttered. "Well, I can't waste any more time. I need full access to the tower and not a word about it to anyone or we will never get to the truth. Confidential!"

Another seven floors up I glimpsed through a side window in the draughty stairshaft the tower rising high above. It was tall with a pointed roof and unforgivably poor stonework. I could see long green drapes billowing from some narrow windows. The Exile States' flag swam coolly from its pole on the tower's lead-capped point. I can't stand that combination of red, white and black or that jagged cross of theirs. "Just you wait," I hissed, "one day the White Star will fly from that pole." I laughed wryly at my own gullibility for entertaining such thoughts. Below me Entwürdigung City's patchwork roofscape spread out in all directions, the odd thread of smoke twining towards the low clouds. I had no time to admire the view though as at that moment a dozen officers descended on me. This was the elite of Rausman's guard, looking fat and happy on what must have been a good lunch.

"Ho! Ho!" said one, a brush of hair across his lip and a monocle embedded into the folds of flesh around his eye. "What have we here?" He wore, like the others, a shining spike-topped helmet on his head and clanking silver and gold medals on his chest. "One of the Buchhalter Kommando! Off the beaten track, rather, aren't we?"

"Grand Officer Hau'ab Schmutztuck. Network code eleven forty one thirty nine. Good day to you, General Befehlnotstand. Please accept my congratulations! Who else could have re-taken Sliabh Eoghann Pass from that rabble regiment, how on earth does one pronounce it? – 'Fine Try'?"

"Ho! Ho! Ho!" bellowed Befehlnotstand. "Come, Officer

Schmutztuck, let us repair to the Smoking Club, it's almost time for the Wire Brandy distribution."

I'd had no problem recognising the old buffoon, his fat red face used to glower at us from every leaf of our Lowland toilet paper, with the caption KNOW YOUR ENEMY below his face. Of course that had all been withdrawn before war broke out. I guess there wasn't much point inciting him unnecessarily in case we lost.

"Investigating the cement case, I presume?" Befehlnotstand and I were by now comfortably installed in our deep armchairs in the Smoking Club, a glass of Wire Brandy and a cigar apiece.

"Yes, amongst other things," I replied casually. "I'm certainly not impressed by the exterior stonework."

"You should see the place from the inside," spluttered Befehlnotstand. "It's an absolute disgrace."

"I fully intend to inspect every inch of it," I said firmly, knocking back a stiff draught of the bitter spirits. "It's a scandal how people waste energy units in wartime."

"Exactly! I share your sentiments entirely. Just look at all the prisoners we've taken and how much we have to spend on them. It's quite ridiculous. Imagine what our City Embellishment Department could do with the money on reconstruction of bridges, embankments and factories. The prisoners should all be shot on sight, not given en suite accommodation. That's what I'd do, but consensus seems impossible here, even on the simplest things!"

"Good point, General," I agreed, beginning to dislike the man. "But I've heard others arguing that we should blow up our own bridges, embankments and factories before the enemy drop their missiles on them; then we wouldn't have to shoot down their machines and take all those costly prisoners."

"Yes, sir. That is Shrumpmann's theory. As you know, Rausman is considering both options. It is apparent, sir, that you are pretty close to the inner circle. Am I right? Ho! Ho! Ho! I knew it! I knew it!"

The assembled company had to drink another bottle of Wire

Brandy but still he showed no sign of stirring so I made my "duty calls" excuses and with a knowing tap on the nose, a click of the heels and a salute plus a final shout of "*Zugang Zurüchschlagen*!" I dived back into the beehive.

If I was lost before I was in a total fog now, what with my bellyfull of spirits. I was pushing my luck and was keen to get on with my business and get the hell out of here.

The anaemic afternoon sun was drowning in the dirty haze and a yellow tinged fog was spreading over the roofscapes as I finally marched towards the new tower and found the mason's workplace on the thirtieth floor at its base.

"Where's the gaffer?" I demanded of a round-bellied stone mason who was bending to pack his tools away.

"Gone 'ome," he replied gloomily, picking up his bag of tools.

"Do you know who I am?" I insisted nastily.

"I do, sir," he shrugged. "You've come about the cement. I told Schlacht the Gaffer, 'No good will come of this, Schlacht,' I said to him. 'They're bound to find out in the end and they'll send in the Buchhalter Kommando and then we'll be in a fine mess.'" He put down his bag and held out his arms. "Put on the cuffs, sir. You will say I co-operated, won't you, sir?"

"First I need to inspect the inside," I said. "Come with me."

"Coming, sir!"

"What cowboys did this plastering, workman?" I demanded, scratching the plaster with my thumbnail. "This will blister in no time."

"My brother Gründlichkeit and I did the plastering, sir."

"Call yourself a craftsman! What a jerry-job! Your name and number!"

"Gotthold Ephraim, Stone Mason of Morgenglocke, sir. Thirteen twenty six forty two. And if it please you, sir, I've never made out that I was a craftsman, sir. But I'm cheap, and that's why the Gaffer gives me work, sir."

"Who lives in this tower, Worker Ephraim?"

"Search me, sir. What's it to me? What with all the changes she keeps making this place won't be ready for another three months at least. Of course with us lot in the dungeon and honest workmen taking over, I suppose it'll all be finished a lot sooner."

"She's a foreigner, the one being kept here, is she not?"

"That abusive little shrew? She's a foreigner all right. And that little brat of hers? Running wild all over the place and dragging his fingers through my wet plasterwork and wasting my time with his silly questions about the city, him and his silly bits of paper. Schlacht the Gaffer sometimes takes him to the punisharium but does he ever learn?"

"So do they still live here?"

"The work has to be finished first, sir."

"Yes, of course. Well, I'm taking you into custody now. It's quite obvious that you're guilty of God knows how many crimes. Head first with you into Rausman's dungeon to rot forever! Have you any family?"

"I have, sir! Thank you for taking them into consideration! Will you take a message to them, sir?"

"That will not be necessary, prisoner. They will be joining you in the dungeon. We cannot allow criminal types of your sort to walk the city streets polluting the atmosphere."

"Quite right, sir."

"But I'm rather tired tonight. I really can't face all the paperwork. Do you know what I think I'll do with you? Instead of Rausman's dungeon for the rest of your life I shall lock you up overnight in the tower. Who's a lucky devil, eh?"

"If it please you, sir, I'm the lucky devil, sir... but, sir, you will still take the wife and kids to the dungeon won't you sir?"

"Yes, yes. Now, go!" And I locked him in the tower and started to grope my way through the gathering shadows towards the stairhead. But the darkness in Entwürdigung Castle is nothing compared to the darkness of Faithful Night's Lower Level and I managed to find my way back to the twentieth floor safely.

Turning a corner I was thrown to the ground by a hurtling bundle of arms and legs and there on the flagstones we thrashed wildly like fish in a net. "All good things must come to an end," I thought to myself as I waited for the click of the searchlights and the crunch of the Heartless Bodies' boots.

"Lemme go! Lemme go!" squealed a high pitched voice from somewhere inside my greatcoat.

"Out from there!" I shouted, catching hold of a stubborn little wrist.

"Not go punisharium. Not go punisharium," wailed the voice plaintively.

"Sorry but the punisharium's the place for you," I said, drawing out the little boy from my coat and pulling him along after me. "You know very well you shouldn't run wild along the corridors. What'll your mother say when she hears?"

"Mum not care. Mum not care." He was struggling and dragging his feet to get away from me.

"Where is your mother at the moment?" I asked as I yanked him after me.

"In our cell. She no come out. I come out."

I was glad to see that his Exilespeak was still pretty basic, but I kept up the pretence in case he guessed who I was.

"Is she alone?"

"No. Rausman with her. Question time."

"Are you allowed out of the castle, Calonnog?"

"No, not out."

"Would you like to be allowed out, instead of going to the punisharium?"

"Yes, go out."

"Fine! Now, what time is your mother expecting you back?"

"After Rausman go. Twenty one hour."

That gave us three hours and I made the most of them. I didn't mean to take the boy away from you, not at all. I had come to take you both away but it's going to be easier next time, I'll know the ropes, you'll be on your own, and the boy far away in a safe place. You'll both have to flee to Small Country, for sure, but you and me will be together again and you'll see that we'll live happy and free up in Small Country and Saffron Tinker and Támé Ingráleat will be there in a cottage in the bowl of the mountains and Faithful Night will welcome us all home. This is how I was thinking as we went down from floor to floor until we reached the foyer with its revolving glass doors. We went out through the back, though; all I had to do was tap in Citizen Architect Ernst Gewalt's network code while the guards thought I was an officer of the Buchhalter Kommando and no one ever smelt a rat; someone even gave Calonnog some sweets which he promptly spat out once we were round the corner.

I didn't bother going back to Providence but went straight to Rausman Central Station to check for westbound trains. Calonnog showed me how to get there, it turned out he knew every twist and turn of the streets. Seems he'd whiled away his time staring down at the city from the castle towers, making little maps of the place and getting the workmen to tell him what was where. There were no passenger trains running but there was a goods train leaving that night, bound for Schadenfreude Forest, so we crept to the far end of the station where the lights grew dim.

Two guards only were on the night train as far as I could see, one up with the stoker and the other riding the tail end. Seems like the energy-saving measures included the railroads. Our train was probably borrowed from the science museum. As she pulled past us I grabbed the connection platform rail and slipped easily on board, Calonnog buttoned inside my greatcoat and his arms clinging around my neck.

"Where are we going, daddy?" piped up Calonnog in our language.

"Home to Lowland, my laddie," I replied. "I'll come back for your mother soon, don't you worry."

"Why can't Mum come with us tonight? She hates that stinky old castle and those fat soldiers."

"How did you know it was me, Calonnog? It's a long time since you and me were together."

"Mum was waiting for you, she said we only had to wait for you. She knew you were coming to fetch us."

"I know, chick," I said, wrapping my coat tighter about him and pushing my fingers through his hair. "I'll soon be back for her." I wedged my boots tight against the wagon's boards and let the rhythmic clanking of the wheels flow through my head. Soon he was sleeping in my arms. On the empty plain between the city and the desert the flames of a burning train shone in his round and perfect face as we sped by.

Testimony Nine

"Well indeed I don't know what to say," said Saffron Tinker, his chin in the cup of his hand at the table where we sat having tea, Calonnog tucking into cream and pancakes prepared by Her Highness Princess Támé Ingráleat-Saffron.

"Well shut up then and say nothing," said the Princess, striking his wrist from under him so that his forehead bounced on the table-top. "Let someone with some sense say something instead."

"You're silly, Uncle Saffron," laughed Calonnog, his cheeks full of pancake.

"I never in my life heard of anyone escaping from Entwürdigung Castle," she continued, "and to cross over into Lowland as well, it's a miracle!"

"I have! I have!" interrupted Saffron Tinker pounding the table and making the saucers tinkle.

"No you haven't for the love of Christ!" she shouted at him and he shut his gob. She turned towards me and said, "It's a pity she's not with us, we wouldn't have a care in the world then."

"Hmmph!" grumbled Saffron Tinker "He'd find something to grouse about, that waste of space that he is, that loser, I'd soon show..."

"Take no notice of him Gwern dear," Támé Ingráleat said, stamping her foot. "Aren't you in enough trouble already, Saffron Tinker?"

"Trouble! Hubble bubble!" he shouted, agitated from head to toe.

"He'd come along so well last time I saw him too," I said.

"This one's like the wind, my love. He can change in a trice. Wait till he's had his tea, you'll see, he'll be fine."

She was right, the tea did the trick and he went out to play with Calonnog in the back garden. You can bet that Saffron Tinker is not a great gardener and his back garden is not much. "My garden" is in fact a patch of slates and nettles behind the cottage. But they also have the rest of the mountain for which Saffron Tinker is not responsible and that looks Ok. Calonnog loves to be with Uncle Saffron wherever he goes, learning all sorts of tricks from him. Saffron Tinker laughs as he listens wide eyed to the boy telling him of life at Entwürdigung Castle.

I'd decided to return to the Exile States at the end of the week but my plans were disrupted by Scarlet Nightshade arriving at the farmyard on her bike this morning. She was nice as cherry pie, said I was looking really well and asked after Saffron Tinker and his wife, did I go to the wedding? I said they were out but come in anyway for a cup of tea. Calonnog had gone with them to the village on the back of his little mule but I didn't mention that to Scarlet Nightshade. She was keeping fine, thanks, but had been through terrible times with the Heartless Bodies, kidnapped by them in fact. None other than Rausman himself had interrogated her – she'd told him nothing, mind – but in the end she'd got herself free and now she was on her way to join up with those Wire Bandits still holed up out in Wild Country, keeping the Exile States at bay. Spies from the Exile States were like flies all over Lowland, see, she said.

"Did you hear anything of Caress then?" I asked her.

"The little tart's only gone over to the enemy, hasn't she; no shame at all, that one! Living like a lady in that dirty old castle and they say she's even exchanged rings with that fat slimy Rausman."

"Who says?" I asked, stunned. "No, I don't believe it."

"Believe what you like, big boy," she said scornfully.

"How are things with Wil Pickled Herring?" I asked, to change the subject.

"Oh he stewed in his own juice way back," she answered evenly. "Serves him right too."

"I thought you two were kind of close."

"Who? Me? With that pisshead? Gwern, where the hell did you get that idea? Anyway, how's tricks with you these days? Heading back to Small Country are we? I bet it's hotting up too much around here for you to hang on much longer."

"I know. You're right."

"So you'll leave Caress in Entwürdigung Castle, then? You're smartening up fast. Listen, I'll come with you up to Small Country. I've got a cousin living there so I can stay without alien status. You and me, Gwern, we go back a long way, it'd be a shame for us to part again, let's go together. You look worn out, dear Gwern, come, lie down. You'll soon feel better, my darling. Take off that big coat..."

Talk about lambs to the slaughter, I told myself weakly as I felt my eyelids droop and she led me by my hand to Saffron Tinker's bedroom.

"Come on, take off your shirt," she said. She was already half undressed, standing before me, a strong-limbed lass, lithe of body, busy with her straps. I was having trouble putting my mind to more serious matters.

"Who's your cousin in Small Country, Scarlet?" I asked.

"I think you probably know quite well who she is," she smiled back.

"What are you suggesting?" I pretended to be innocent.

"You used her! You threw her away like a used up ragdoll... But, hey, she always was a cheap little bitch and she got what was coming so who gives a toss?"

"And you're not using me now?" I felt like I could see through her like rain. "You don't seem to mind getting cosy round the fireplace with Caress, do you, telling stories about me, you spiteful slag."

"You two-faced sleazeball yourself," she spat. "She deserved to know what you're really like, you two-timing bastard. You had it coming way off."

"And what are you really like, then, Scarlet Nightshade? With your tales to Caress and more tales to Fischermädchen. She tells tales to Befehlnotstand and he tells the Heartless Bodies. It's called a chain of command, I'm told. You're just a treacherous bitch!"

"Ha! Ha! Ha!" she laughed as she stooped and straightened again with a shining razor blade in her hand. "Well, who's a clever boy then? Too clever by half I'd say. Even Caress won't want you when I've sliced you up like a side of bacon, sonny!" She lunged at me and drew the blade lightly through the thick of my naked forearm, opening it up like a pig's throat. The blood gushed over the bed-sheets as she drew back and came at me again but I rolled aside and caught her wrist in my left hand, pressing down on the back of her hand until the blade dropped from her grasp and I grabbed it.

"Try one more dirty trick like that," I snarled, holding the blade right in front of her eyes, "and I'll cut you up into pieces too small for even the crows. Now, get dressed and get out!"

I know I shouldn't have let her go. Killing a spy would've been the only option for a professional soldier. I just couldn't do it though, couldn't even think of doing that. She was too alive, too fine, and too close, not like those ants we wiped out on the reservoir embankment. And I couldn't keep her there either, even as a prisoner, or she would've known Calonnog was here and she'd have got word out about him somehow.

So away she went on her bike as I stood on the threshold, the blood rusting on the razor blade in my hand and the stain creeping through the rag on my arm.

That was this morning. Now I've got to go. Back to Entwürdigung City before she gets back to base and brings the sky down about my head. At least the network screen works in this house. This copy is for you, Caress. There is no blood on it, she missed my artery. I have a couple of stiches. I left Saffron Tinker, Támé Ingráleat and Calonnog a message on the table.

See you in a day or two. Scarlet Nightshade was here but knows nothing about Calonnog. I attach in a separate file my mobile processor data, hope there's nothing too bad in it about Saffron Tinker. See you,

Gwern

In Zählappell's apartment the word machine clicked once and loaded the second word file into play. Having been up all the previous night Zählappell was snoozing happily in his comfy armchair and noticed nothing as the screen lit up and the second file began to scroll its text up the screen:

Testimony Ten

Gwern, darling, why did you come to fetch us? Now I've got two holes in my heart instead of one. Rausman says you were no better than a highwayman. A thieving rebel. He likes to toy with the replay button as he shows me his compilation of surveillance footage and interrogation. "That stupid little worm," he calls you. He's a swine of a man, but I've got to keep up appearances or my life wouldn't be worth living. Is it worth living anyway, I wonder? Is it true that I won't see you again, Gwern?

Scarlet Nightshade comes to see me of an afternoon and she never fails to taunt me about your unfaithfulness. She gloats about how close you were to her cousin in the Small Country. She said you had an affair with her in Saffron Tinker's cottage in Lowland. I never took too much notice of Scarlet Nightshade's wild rantings, I knew it was not all true. I remember Scarlet Nightshade at Helen's Stone telling me all sorts of bad things about you. I always thought she was in love with you but you never acknowledged it. I suppose you didn't love her back enough, I don't think you loved her at all. Anyway it turned to hate in her against you and she went to work for Fischermädchen. I know that's why they came for me and Calonnog. I know that's why we were given this so-called luxurious tower in the capital city of the Exile States. Calonnog was my world and when he was lost my world became cold. No-one knew or no-one would tell me where he'd gone. I thought it was one of Rausman's tricks to get me to eat or sleep. Where is Calonnog, Gwern? Is he with Saffron Tinker? Have they tried to reach Small Country? I know all the paths are closed now between Lowland and Small Country and I'm sick with worrying what's happened. Poor Calonnog. If only I could know what happened. And if they were caught by Befehlnotstand did he kill them as he kills all his captives? Or were they taken by the Heartless Bodies and are right now on their way to Entwürdigung City. Or are they here already in some underground cell shivering and calling out for the light? If you were alive you could tell me, Gwern, my darling, but now I have no place left to turn.

Gwern, my true love and friend, they have raised your poor head on a pole by the castle gates; Rausman says I must go to look at you but I will not. He's such a cruel man, Gwern, he has so many ways to hurt me. He gets a kick out of hauling that brute Befehlnotstand up here to the tower and he says to him, "Explain to us again how you killed that thieving little fox."

And the fat giant starts to boast about how they surrounded you by the banks of Häfling River, where it turns from Schadenfreude Forest towards Entwürdigung City, on a cold late afternoon as the sun sank low over the blood red river. There you were on the back of your mule which they shot from under you and then they had some fun with you until they got tired of it and killed you like a worm before retiring to their tents for the night. They're saying now you were nothing but a snivelling coward and that the new legends about you are way off the mark – you were just a little piece of dirt, pleading for your life, willing to implicate anyone. I never believed that bastard Befehlnotstand and I don't believe it.

I wish you'd come again into my dreams, Gwern. Come tonight, please. Let me feel you are close again before it gets dark.

Your Caress

The word machine gave another click as the third file activated. The sound stirred Zählappell slightly in his dream. He dreamt he was alone in the network Screen Archives late at night, selecting at random all the files that he could carry and loading them one by one into the banks of screens that filled the floor until the whole chamber was a multi-coloured place of voice and movement all together. The click did not wake him and he didn't therefore notice the following words that were moving up across his screen:

Testimony Eleven

Gwern Excuses, the boy is pulling the house down around our ears. Her indoors and me, we're so old and feeble now we can't catch up with the little monkey all day. I won't deny he's a dear one, though. He loves it up here in the pure Small Country air. Some workmen from New Village came to help me build a little cottage on the site of my old hut up in the crook of the hills, cozy as a nest. You know, we were lucky to get here at all, Gwern, the way these guys travel light. The last path was closed soon after we crossed over. I don't think it was a coincidence. Mind you, with my connections... we were lucky we even got close. But it's fine here now, Gwern, Spring is blue on the hillsides and the songbirds are out early with their song. All you have to do is imagine that the mules are lambs and you can feel as if you're back in Lowland once again.

It's been a hard blow for Faithful Night, Gwern. You know that both he and the Answer Keeper had thought you'd stand in the breach at the eleventh hour when it came. They did not account for the fact that you'd be dead. I should have been pushing up the daisies long ago, but even an old fool like me misses you, bright flower; when I think those devils took you apart in cold blood it makes my blood churn until things swim before my eyes and I get mad again. I want to sweep my arms across the tables, breaking everything within reach, I'm so mad I go outside and shout "Gwern!" from the high pastures, I shout "Gwern!" as I stumble through the wooded slopes. I whisper "Gwern," on my knees with my ear to the mouth of the mountain stream and her indoors says I've lost my marbles, wants me back down the Lower Level but I won't go.

I want to see our boy racing his little mule and I'll help him build a tree house in the ash behind the house and I watch the light in his eyes when he sees something new. I say to myself, "Calm down, Saffron Tinker." Támé Ingráleat and I will bring up the boy for Caress and you; one day I'll tell him what happened that frozen night on the banks of the Häfling River. I'll tell him how soon it took Scarlet Nightshade to tell them where to wait for you. How they shot your mule from under you, how you kept the Heartless Bodies at bay until they shot you down and your blood ran red into the river and they cut off your head and stuck it on a pole on Entwürdigung Castle where the crows peck at your head above the castle gate. I'll give him your mobile processor data and Calonnog will be your worthy heir, Gwern. Someone is going to pay for this violence, in the name of God, their hour of vengeance will come.

I'm beginning to get worked up again, Gwern. I'm trying to avoid negative and aggressive thoughts, especially both together. I'd better close down for now. Until tomorrow

Saffron Tinker

It's me again, Gwern, just back with Calonnog from a walk above New Village this afternoon. You remember, where Pilgrim World used to knock on a stone door. We were summoned to the Lower Level by, you guessed it, Faithful Night. "You won't be afraid of the dark, will you?" I said to the little one. "No, not as scared as you, anyway," he said. "Grandpa," he asked, "what's that big wooden door in the cliffside?" "That's the Door of Answers, Calonnog, and you must never touch..." Of course before I could finish, the rascal had run away from me and was tugging at the steel hoop that hung down as a handle. On oiled runners the big oak doors slipped aside and the afternoon sun's rays flooded through the Door of Answers and the voice of the Answer Keeper came quietly from within, "Welcome, Calonnog, the time has come."

Everything has been arranged, Gwern! He's going to stay with us until he's old enough to start with Faithful Night and then he'll go to live in the Lower Level to study at the feet of the Answer Keeper himself! Lower Level is a sea of light now, Gwern, not a black hole as it used to be, and Faithful Night is all smiles now. He's a little man like myself, Gwern, he wears a suit of homespun cloth and calf skin shoes and he smokes a pipe, Gwern, can you believe it? I haven't met the Answer Keeper but I bet he's just as friendly too.

No news from Entwürdigung City, I'm afraid. But Faithful Night promises to help us bring back Caress from her lonely tower. I've told him I'm coming out of retirement and I'm going to find her. What do you think of that, Gwern? Do you remember how I found you when you were in the Exile States? Old Saffron Tinker will do it again, Gwern, and if I die trying, who cares? Támé Ingráleat-Saffron even wants to come with me! We'll have to wait until Calonnog is old enough to go alone to the Lower Level, but there are only a few years until then.

The word machine was bleeping like a watch alarm and flashing the message, "END" in large green letters across the screen. The clerk Zählappell woke up and stretched over to turn it off. "Oh, shit," he groaned, "another night in the chair. Just my luck to get some old fashioned crap about the war. Why can't I be like that jammy sub-archivist, Windesharfe? He got some word and picture cards with naked girls, full colour, 360 degrees."

He got up stiffly and pushed the curtains to one side. The grey morning was unwinding the knots of cloud around the castle ramparts and the River Häfling was like lead below. Only a few windows showed yellow against the castle's dark walls. The clouds parted briefly to reveal the white star straining in the wind on its pole on the pointed roof of the highest tower.

"What sort of time is this? Oh, to hell with it!" Zählappell was already cursing the start of his day when there came a loud rapping at his door.

The Artist

Elfyn Lewis was born in Porthmadog in 1969. His distinctive large-scale, abstract canvasses appear in a number of public and private collections. His work has been successful in crossing cultural and art-form boundaries appearing as album and book covers as well as making an impact at galleries and exhibitions around the world. For further information: www.elfynlewis.com